I0526599

My Ascent Into Submission

First Edition

Published by The Nazca Plains Corporation
Las Vegas, Nevada
2011

ISBN: 978-1-61098-216-0
E-book: 978-1-61098-217-7

Published by

The Nazca Plains Corporation ®
4640 Paradise Rd, Suite 141
Las Vegas NV 89109-8000

PUBLISHER'S NOTE
My Ascent Into Submission is a work of fiction created wholly by
Nick Williams' imagination. All characters are fictional and any
resemblance to any persons living or deceased is purely by accident.
No portion of this book reflects any real person or events.

Cover Photos
Ladder, PixBox
Man, Ulia Koltyrina

Art Director
Blake Stephens

My Ascent Into Submission

First Edition

Nick Williams

DEDICATION

This book is dedicated to my SIR

CONTENTS

CONTENT CONTINUED

CHAPTER ONE

My Ascent

Before I can tell you about the juicy steamy erotic parts of my ascent to submission, and there are a lot of scenes, it's necessary for you to know where I came from before this transformation occurred. It took a lot of work, mentally, emotionally, and physically to get to this place. Some might call it a recovery or a reclaiming of my identity. Either way, it didn't happen overnight. Only from this starting point can you comprehend the desire, the pleasure and commitment that went into the climb up.

At first, my friends didn't understand why I sold my house of 20 years and moved away from the serene Russian River. It's the house I had bought in 1984, with my partner, who died shortly thereafter. The house that I thought I would die in. But one thing that I have finally learned is that some things are out of our control. Life takes many turns, and dying didn't happen.

I had heard others say that after a loss, or some other trauma, they had to move, to move on. I guess it took me a little longer to come to these sentiments. I tried making a life for myself in the old house. Some aspects worked. I became an avid gardener, a published writer and an established and respected political activist. These things brought me deep personal satisfaction for many years. But other quality-of-life aspects never came to fruition. One of them was a genuine connection with another man. And as the calendar pages flipped, it became apparent that changes had come to the Russian River. The heydays were long gone. Although it's only one and a half hours from San Francisco, it had become a place to bring a boyfriend, not find one.

This desire for companionship gave me motivation to let go of the past. One morning after sharing with my therapist how lonely it felt living along the Russian River he told me to stop off at a realtor and ask about selling my house. Upon leaving the office I took his advice.

It wasn't an easy choice or an easy task. But I surrounded myself with people who supported my decision. Family members flew out and cleaned my house before it went on the market. I didn't know the kitchen floor was purple until my sister-in-law washed it with ammonia. My brother fixed hinges and windows and molding. A month later, when the house sold, another brother and his wife flew out to pack up and empty the house. I was still so attached to many of the old things, his things, the knick knacks and tables, the paintings and books, that they ordered me to leave the house and let them decide what to pack up. What didn't need to go into storage they sold in the yard sale that they also organized. It tore me apart to see strangers squabbling over his things for a few dollars. Luckily and fortunately, I knew enough not to impede our momentum. On the day I turned the keys in to the realtor, I said good bye to the home that had nurtured me and thanked the trees that had sheltered me and farewell to the river that had soothed me.

With the new house in Palm Springs still in escrow I spent a couple of weeks in San Francisco. September is my favorite month there. The fog recedes and the weather warms. A friend convinced me to have silicone injections to restore my face. Though I had survived and thrived, thirty three years of HIV had left its toll. I hated looking at myself in the mirror and I hated seeing pictures of myself even more. But what he was suggesting seemed extravagant, bourgeois, and shallow.

"I've done it for three years. It's safe and it works. We're used to people looking at us because we're hot. Not because we're deformed," he told me.

His advice stayed with me. If I were going to leave Monte Rio, the little town along the river where our house was, it had to be all or nothing. I made an appointment with the doctor he recommended. A friend went along with me for support. Having never done anything like this before I was excited and terrified. As the doctor stood above me with a syringe in his hand ready to stick in my face 50 or 60 times, I grabbed his shirt and said, "Don't make a mistake."

He stopped. "What kind of mistake do you think I'll make?"

"I just keep thinking I'm gonna come out looking bruised and deformed."

"You are going to look great. You're a handsome guy. You're going to thank me when it's done."

He was right. My face came back to an acceptable appearance. Sure I might not look 25 anymore but the figure in the mirror didn't make me ill. My self-image was restored and my confidence grew. Two things in my life had changed.

The move was exhausting. Once the moving truck was emptied in Palm Springs and delivered back to U-Haul I didn't venture far from the house. With my own energy depleted I still faced five rooms of boxes. In earlier years I would have celebrated my new life by hanging out at the resorts and going out to the bars at night. Now, well into my 40's I knew it was more important in the long run to get my home life in order. I hated to admit it, but I was finally at that age when a calm peaceful place to live was necessary before I could focus on other needs. Even the gym took second place in importance to setting up a house.

A good day was spent unpacking, peeling the old wall paper, picking out colors and painting the walls. Trips to Lowes, Home Depot, and Builders Supply took time and energy. Of course this activity was exhausting, but on a deep level it felt good to be taking care of myself in this way rather than depending on others to do it for me as I had in my younger years where a smile could get me what I wanted.

Though not a perfectionist by any means, I didn't even tape around the windows, I still wanted my new home to mirror the new me. The inside does reflect on the outside and I was ready to look good again. Back on the Russian River, protected by the shade of over a hundred towering redwoods, life had been about going inward and healing from the grief and loss. The interior walls were basic white; clothes were dirty jeans, tee shirts and flannel shirts. Now I was ready for something different. I wanted cheery and lively colors so I chose gold and yellow frost for the living room and mango for my bedroom. I kept a sure and steady pace, moving from one room to the other.

When the interior was acceptable, I tackled the gravelly barren yard.

Luckily, the desert heat had released its grip and the weather had dropped below triple digits. The elderly woman I bought the house from wanted no maintenance. That wouldn't work for me. Having cultivated a rich and rewarding shade garden in the old house, I knew the pleasures a garden brings. The familiar Fuchsias and Begonias, shade loving plants I was accustomed to on the River, would not survive the fierce desert sun.

I was going to have to relearn it all. The first stop for this project was the local library to find desert gardening books. I had to learn about the plants I liked, how fast they grew, how much water they required and the best location to place them. Then discover where to buy the plants and determine what size to buy.

There were several trips to the desert oriented nursery at the Living Desert, a wildlife and botanical park about twenty miles from the house. There were trips to other nurseries in the area as well, and many back to Lowe's. Slowly, the garden took form. There were Ocotillos, with skeleton looking unbranched thorny canes that grow 10 feet tall. After a rain, little green leaves shoot out from the canes and spikes of orange flowers explode from the top to the delight of hummingbirds, bees and humans. There were Louellas or Wild Petunias, and my favorite name – Baja Fairy Duster, with pink and red puffball flowers with long stamens. Certainly I knew it would take several seasons for things to grow in and the magic to show.

At Christmas, since I was single and didn't have that special someone to unwrap presents with, and since I was still so new to the desert that I hadn't yet made a family of friends, I decided this was an opportunity to visit my family in New England. It had been a decade since the last trip back for the holiday and they were so helpful with the move it felt like the right thing to do. The weather, fortunately, stayed mild and the visit went well.

I returned to the desert for the New Year full of optimism for the next phase of my new life. Unfortunately, the second day home, I ended up at the emergency room with a 103 fever. I must have picked up an infection on the plane. After four hours of fluids and meds the fever subsided and the hospital released me.

I was determined not to let this setback alter my plans. It took a week before I could pick up a shovel to dig and a few days longer for me to feel strong enough to start to the gym. My body was sore after that first workout, as it should be. The third night back into my routine I felt strong enough to up the weights. I approached my favorite exercise, the one that had always given me admired pecs – the incline bench, with determination. The first set went well. But on the second set something gave out and tightness gripped my shoulder.

Over the next few days the tightness seemed to intensify. By the evening my body was tired and sore. At times, I actually felt sick and took a couple of days off from doing anything, even in the garden. Days turned into weeks. Returning to the gym was not possible. This latest setback affected me emotionally. For the first time, doubt crept in and I wondered if the move had been a mistake.

Dating seemed like a ritual unavailable to me. Even making friends seemed like too much work in my current condition.

But it was too soon to give in. I had worked too hard getting this far. It was evident that the move was still impacting me so I continued to go slow, giving my body ample time to recover, doing minor projects around the house and spending time with the dog. Finally, with perseverance and enough time the soreness in my body subsided.

That's when other priorities and desires took on more urgency. I ventured out into the dating world of Palm Springs but it didn't take long to discover that I had traded one small River town for a couples-oriented retirement home. There were lots of guys available for sex but not many for dating. NSA – no strings attached is not what I was searching for. The move was about getting what I wanted; about quality of life. I knew deep in my gut and in my heart that I was ready for something real and gratifying. But how I would get that remained elusive.

So I joined several clubs and support groups in hopes that this would lead to a few dates. But this too led to dead ends. Nice guys but not what I wanted. Of course, it would help to know what it was that I was looking for. I couldn't quite put my finger on it. I just knew I wanted someone different. This time it had to change. That's what the move was all about. I wanted to be overwhelmed.

Occasionally, I searched the chat lines on AOL or the sex lines such as Men4SexNow. But most times my effort was futile and the results disappointing. On rarer nights I actually went out to a couple of the bars. But it's not a good idea to go out and be seen yawning.

My frustration level grew so I chose to go back into therapy in an attempt to understand why I still wasn't getting what I wanted. I imagined just moving would be enough. That as soon as I was here, my guy in shining armor would appear. I couldn't help but think that something still wasn't right. Like a detective I was determined to figure it out.

After listening to me each week my therapist's response was always, "Be patient." He said it over and over again. And he also asked me, "What do you want?"

"What do I want?" I mumbled to myself.

So I said to him, "I know this might sound silly but when I've had a rough day I want to lay my head on a hairy chest. I want to rub my face in a big man's beard. After I've shot my load I want him to fuck me some more."

"You a want a daddy," he said, chuckling.

"How about big brother?"

"Is that how it was with your partner who died?"

"Yes," I said, nodding.

"You can have that again," he assured me. "Be patient. You just moved here."

Then, a friend turned me on to this web site, WorldLeathermen. He said there were lots of guys from Palm Springs on it and that I should check it out.

So I took his advice. The site seemed serious. The ads were graphic, explicit. These guys weren't just standing and modeling. They were hot and ready. They seemed to know what they wanted. They were looking for sex. Intense sex. I quickly wrote up a profile for myself and got a friend to take a picture of me with my shirt off to upload. It wasn't a good picture but it was a start. Each night I checked out the site, to make sure I wanted to become a full paying member. I contacted some guys. The responses were not good. This was a leather site and I realized I was the one who wasn't prepared. I was the one without leather, without graphic pictures.

How determined was I to get what I wanted? What kind of compromises to my principles would I make to get it? What sacrifices would I accept? Most of my leather was still in boxes. In mothballs. I had determined that my leather was for an era when I was younger, hotter.

I took out the box storing my gear and tried it on. The man in the mirror didn't look so bad. I had my roommate take more pictures. Back online I took the initiative and contacted several handsome men. The response improved. Some were willing to hookup, but for my own emotional safety, I had made a decision to not play with coupled men, which in Palm Springs eliminated a lot of them.

As I perused the ads I found myself drawn to the tops. As I opened to the idea of the possibility of getting fucked, again, on a regular basis my mind expanded. After a decade of being in control out of fear, I was ready to answer the question – What did I REALLY want?

I decided to take a risk and go all out. Some people say they don't have a type. Or they like all types. I had a type and I knew what worked for me. I had experimented long enough. I had compromised and accommodated nice guys. It was time to go back to my primal desires. I had deliberately avoided it for long enough. I wanted the opposite of me. Being smooth I wanted a hairy guy. Being slender I wanted a beefy guy and a taller guy. Being smart and educated I wanted someone more intellectual and more well-read. And I wanted it rough.

I changed my profile to express these dormant desires. Smooth Muscle guy for Bigger Hairy DOM. I expanded my search area to include LA and San Diego and Phoenix.

In the evenings I searched online for possibilities. I wanted someone with experience. The guys in full leather were hot, the ones professing to only play in full leather, were intriguing. And I did want leather sex routinely and regularly back in my life but I also knew that for me, ultimately, the guy had to be able to take it off and still function at the gym, political events, the dog park, the beach, or by the pool. Leather was an accessory, an important one, of course, but it didn't make the man. The man made the leather. Masculinity doesn't happen when the cow hide goes on. It's got to already be there.

Changes were happening in other areas of my life. I finally joined World Gym. Gold's was good and the lighting and the view outside their huge wall of glass was spectacular but I was tired of all the uptight young hets. Most of the gay guys had already migrated over to World.

It had been years since I belonged to a predominantly gay gym. In some respects it can be as intimidating as joining a Venice Beach gym. The cruising, the gossip, the shower room, the chatty guys. It can be enough to make one rush back to hide out in the safe confines of a straight gym.

My first day there I made sure was during the calmer time of the afternoon. I would do this slowly. It brought back memories of The Muscle System in San Francisco when I was younger, during the carefree years of the early 80's. The years when walking into a gym were as easy as walking into a grocery store. No doubts. No fears. I owned the place. Of course it was with the dozen or so other guys who also had the same attitude. On warm days we worked out with our shirts off.

Turned out it was an easy adjustment. That's not to say I didn't feel some intimidation. That I didn't experience moments of insecurities. But when those emotions surfaced I dove deeper into my workout. My body felt good for the first time in many years. My energy had returned and maybe the move transition was behind me.

After a few days faces became familiar and I recognized some of the guys from the dog park. As the weeks went by, I slowly increased the weights. My body adjusted and I could see the changes. I also noticed there were a lot of trainers around this gym. More than I'd ever seen anywhere else. I'd never used a trainer before, even when I first started out. I had played sports and it came naturally to me. But a nagging image stayed with me. What if I got hurt again? All the plans and dreams could be for naught. Then it occurred to me, I didn't have to do it the same way I had always done it. I didn't have to do my recovery alone. I could to get help. After selling my house, I wasn't cash poor anymore. I had moved for a better quality of life. Getting hurt would not bring me that quality I was after.

But how do you choose a trainer? I didn't want to pick one just because he was handsome or big either. So after watching a few of them over several weeks I took a chance and chose one who seemed serious but not too serious. Who was involved with his clients but not too overbearing. He was big but not too big. Alright, he was handsome, too. That helped. And yes, he happened to be hairy. Exactly how I wanted to look. Maybe that is how you choose a trainer. We set up a time for an interview.

"I'm not one of those guys with a lot of money." I said, upfront.

"Not all my clients stay with me. A few do. Most don't. Some live in other cities and I only see them when they're here," he said. "We specialize in guys over 40."

I liked hearing that. "Do you think I can get bigger?"

"Absolutely. I know you will."

He said the right words about nutrition and rest and not hurting myself and still getting bigger and looking better. "I've watched you work out. You're here every day. You do too much. You don't give your body enough time to recover. I forbid you to enter the gym on your days off."

I was startled.

It must have shown because he smiled at my reaction. "I know you'll do too much. You're not thirty any more. And I'm putting you on a high protein diet."

Maybe I wasn't as smart as I thought I was.

We agreed on a three week course and then I would go on my own. Before the first workout he opened a notebook with my name on it to keep track of my sets. He insisted I carry a bench towel. I felt foolish the first few sessions. What was I doing with a trainer? After all these years on my own had I become one of those old guys who couldn't do it for themselves? One of those guys I had scorned and avoided in my youth.

But after over a decade of worrying about getting sick if I pushed too hard and now concerned about injuries, I knew deep down inside it was for the best. I wanted to be pushed and he pushed me hard.

He chose eight different exercises at four and five reps. We did full body workouts every other day. The workouts were excruciating. My body ached and after some food I crashed on the couch for two hours.

"I want you to promise me that you'll continue to work out hard," he said as he handed me my workout book at the end of the three weeks.

"You know I will," I answered.

"I know you will," he responded, "that's why I was happy to take you on and made room for you in my schedule. Feel free to ask me any questions. I'd like you to remain on this routine for three months then let's talk about where to go from there."

We shook hands and he departed.

It didn't take long for the results to show. I could see my body change. The number on the scale slowly ticked up, passing 175 in a matter of a few weeks. I had never weighed more. Not since after I had graduated from college, when I worked six nights as a waiter and attended classes all day, had I gained weight so fast. I still remember the jubilation that summer when I passed 160 pounds. I hated being a skinny kid and always wanted to be bigger. I was ecstatic to see the numbers rise again. My chest bulked up like boulders and my biceps nearly doubled. Muscled guys who had previously ignored me started saying hello. Some of them even followed me into the locker room. I caught them watching me undress. I couldn't wait to get back to the gym for my next workout.

It seemed I had my answer to all the sleepless nights wondering if moving was a good decision. This was more positive tangible evidence on my new personal life.

CHAPTER TWO

Always Call ME SIR

My usual message to the guys I found attractive was simple. "Nice pecs. Like your hairy chest. Ever get out here to the desert?"

Most would respond back to tell me they did and would let me know when it was going to happen.

"Tell ME what your experiences are," one reply from a SIRManTop read. "And always address ME as SIR."

His words piqued my curiosity and I repeated his demand out loud. "Always address ME as SIR." I'd never called anyone SIR before but felt an immediate tightening sensation in my chest. The first part of his comeback was an original twist on the dreaded, "what are you into?" How I hated that question since there never was a simple answer. Coming of age in San Francisco in the 70's you tried everything. Very few things were off limits or taboo. At least that's how it was for me. If a guy was hot you just did it.

When I clicked on this profile the caption read "Nasty verbal SIR". SIRManTop was from LA. He wore a ball cap and was glancing downward so I couldn't get a good look at his face. He had a tank top on that showed off big developed biceps with a tattoo circling the left one but I wasn't able to make out what it was. He definitely had a hairy body and a muscular chest. It read that he was 100 percent active and that he was looking for guys willing to serve and be trained. His height was six feet one inch tall. It said that he was a passionate and respectful master. And that his age was 45.

"Always refer to ME as SIR." I repeated it again wondering why HE capitalized the ME. Maybe for emphasis. You learn to take these profiles with a grain of desert sand but this one grabbed my attention. Most people lie about their age, sometimes by ten years. Some put pictures that are ten years old. The Worldleathermen site wasn't like AOL or some of the other web sites. It didn't have a chat room then. When you initiated contact with someone you never knew if or when the other person was going to get back to you. You hoped they checked their mail once a day.

There's always a risk in communicating back. A couple of short sentences might give the impression that you aren't too interested. By saying too much you can sound chatty and lose his interest.

"I've done a lot," I wrote. "I hope I can get enough across without going on too long. I like the basics. Sucking and fucking." I thought about what else to say. How much info do you give a stranger? How much time do you spend on a guy you may never hear from again?

Continuing, I wrote, "Sometimes I like bondage. I love my nipples played with. I've done some rimming. Dirty armpits are like a hit of poppers. I have a sling and sometimes I used to get into fisting and dildos. I like my chest punched and my stomach slugged. One guy punched my legs and biceps. That was hot. I've done some flogging and had a caning stick used on me once. Paddles, belts on my ass. I like hand marks on my ass. I hope this is what you were looking for. If you want to know anything else just ask. I'm open to trying new things."

I read and reread my words. Did I cover enough? Did it make sense? Any misspelled words? I hated getting mail with misspelled words. Not that I'm a word snob but if a person can't take the time to check for spelling, what does that say about him. I checked through my reply one more time then realized I hadn't put "SIR" at the beginning. Don't want to make any mistakes so soon. I wrote "SIR" at the beginning and clicked Send.

It took a day for SIRManTop to respond. "Do you live alone?" Do you have a playroom? And from now on never disrespect ME. Always capitalize any reference to ME. Understood?"

Whoa! I thought as I read HIS mandate. "Always capitalize any reference to ME," I said it out loud to make sure I comprehended it correctly. No comment on the things I wrote. Just capitalize any reference to HIM; I said this silently to myself. What kind of a guy is this?

"I have a roommate. He goes to sleep early. I can bring people home. But even better, he owns a resort in town. I can get a room over there. All the rooms have hooks in the ceiling," I wrote back.

The next day this had arrived from SIRManTop."How rough do you get? When was the last time?"

Not a man of many words, I thought, after reading HIS questions.

"Last November I met a guy from San Diego. He punched me so hard he left bruises on my chest that scabbed over the next week."

A day later. "That's the last time you played rough? In November?" SIRManTop wrote.

It was now April. I didn't tell him about my moving situation or about getting sick or the shoulder injury. It was too much information. HE would probably lose interest, so I wrote. "I can't find guys out here in PS to hit me the way I like it."

The next day he wrote back, "There are a lot of guys out there who play rough."

"Most of them are married. I don't play with married guys. Just something I decided for myself. Are you single?" This is usually the deal breaking question. So many times I'd meet a handsome masculine guy and they would already be in a relationship. I eagerly anticipated seeing what his answer would be.

"Single." It stated the following morning. "Send ME your number and tell ME when the best time to call you is."

Because of the doubting Thomas in me I didn't really put credence in HIS plan to talk. Experience showed that people lied and that HE wouldn't call even though HE seemed interested. I figured it was a brush off but I sent back my number and told HIM a good time to try.

Wednesday evening the phone rang. "This is SIR, from the leather site," a deep smooth voice said. It took me a few seconds to recollect about the leather site and who I had met. "I told you I would call you today."

Now I was focused. HE had told me he would. This one keeps HIS promises, I thought. "Yes SIR. That's right. I'm glad you called. How are you?" I hoped it wouldn't show how nervous I was.

"Tell me about this room at your friend's resort. What's the name of it?" HIS voice was calm showing no sign of nervousness on his part.

"It's Camp Palm Springs. In the north end of town. It's a clean place with lots of palm trees. It's got 29 rooms. They're all nicely furnished. All the rooms on the second floor have hooks in the ceiling for slings. Or just use the hooks with chains. It's a fun place."

"How often can you get a room?" The masculine sound of HIS voice turned me on.

"Anytime they aren't sold out. Haven't gotten a room in a while."

"How come it's been so long since you played rough? Don't you like it?"

"No, I like it. Just don't meet many guys here. They're all married. I don't like playin' with married guys. This last guy was from San Diego. He was over here for the weekend. We met online." I hoped I wasn't sounding whiny.

"How was it? What did he do to you?"

"It was good. Pretty intense. He punched my chest as hard as he could. Left some nice bruises. Hardest anyone has hit me so far. The bruises even scabbed over and peeled. The guy came four times. I liked it. I'd do it again but our schedules just haven't gotten together."

"Did you get a room then?"

"No, he had a room at The Villas. We met up at a bar and then went to his room."

"Did he tie you up?"

"No, we didn't get into that. Just punchin' and fuckin'."

"No flogging?"

"He had a little one but it looked like a toy. He just used his fist."

"I play rough. You think you can handle it?"

"I'll do the best I can." I could tell my voice rose a bit on the last word.

"What equipment do you have?"

"I just bought some wrist restraints over at Gear Leather, the leather shop in town. Haven't used them, yet. I bought some new tit clamps there, also. I have one flogger, a leather paddle, handcuffs, clothespins."

"What are your limits?"

"My limits?" Here it was again. That question. What are you into? What are your limits? I took a deep breath before answering. "I don't know. It's different with each guy. It changes all the time. There isn't anything I can think of that I won't do. I am HIV positive. I should get that out of the way. Is that a problem for you?"

"No, I've been with positive guys. We won't be doing any fucking. Just S and M. I want to see how much you can take. My only limit is blood. There'll be no blood."

"OK. That's fine with me," I replied.

"How soon can you get a room? Can you get one for this weekend?"

HIS quickness to visit brought a smile to my face. I checked the calendar on my wall. "No, this weekend isn't good. They have their play parties on the first weekend of every month. They'll be sold out so I can't get a room. The following weekend works. I can get a room then."

"I can get out there next Saturday. Get the room and I'll talk to you later next week and give you instructions on how I want things."

"Sounds good to me. Nice talking with YOU." We hung up.

It was the best interaction I'd had in a long time. Now we would see if it really happened.

The heat took hold of the desert early that week and the citrus blossoms exploded into full bloom. The scent filled the cool dry evening air with a sweet aroma that sent my sinuses into overdrive. It gripped my head like a vise, I couldn't breathe, and my throat hurt, putting my workouts on hold for few days until my ENT (ear, nose and throat) doc could get things under control. I worried that my luck had run out and that infections would resume.

I hoped my new friend, SIR, wouldn't call. I didn't want HIM to think I was canceling on HIM. It didn't look like this sinus thing was going to break in time for the weekend. Thursday morning I fretted, wondering all day if HE'd call. I hoped HE wouldn't and I hoped HE would. By nightfall, still feeling achy, I climbed into bed early and figured the call wasn't going to happen. A short time later, the phone rang.

"It's SIR. What are you doing?"

HIS voice was low and masculine. It was exciting to hear it. "I'm in bed watching TV."

"You're in bed already?" There was definite surprise in HIS voice.

"I know, it's early, but I'm watching TV. I'm not going to sleep yet."

"Did you get a room?"

"I did. But I'm not sure it's going to work out."

"Why not? You afraid?"

This made me chuckle. "No, I'm not afraid. I haven't felt good. Spring is here in the desert and my sinuses have gotten infected. I feel weak. I'm not sure my body is ready for any abuse."

"We shouldn't do this if you aren't feeling good. I want you full of energy when I beat you."

"I agree. I don't want you thinking I'm canceling because I'm not interested."

It was HIS turn to laugh. "I don't worry about that. Why don't you call me when you're better and I'll come out then?"

"I'm sorry about this. I was looking forward to it."

"Call me when you're better." HE hung up.

I figured that was it. Dead. No way to salvage this. HE thinks I've blown him off. I would think the same way. It took a few more days for the meds and rinses to clear out the infection. I started back on my workout routine at half the weights. By the end of the following week I was back in full force and ready to push some limits. HE had told me to call HIM when I was better but calling HIM out of the blue made me uncomfortable. What if HE didn't remember me? Or HE changed his mind? Contacting HIM online felt safer.

"The infection's gone. I'm ready for you now, SIR," I wrote to SIRManTop.

I certainly didn't expect to hear from HIM instantly but after a few days went by and still not a word I figured HE had lost interest. But there were other guys to cruise. Other opportunities to search out. Frustratingly, not much happened on the local scene. The guys in PS just weren't clicking so getting to the gym took precedent and the scale continued to tip up, pound by pound, creeping toward 180. My favorite time to work out was around 1pm when my energy and strength were at their peak. This gave me ample time to get to appointments and run around and do any errands that might need to get done. I felt fortunate to not have to wait until after work.

The weather continued to hit triple digits as May came around.

One evening the phone rang. "I've been expecting to hear from you," a deep voice said.

"It didn't feel right calling YOU. I'm glad YOU called."

"You feeling better?"

"I am. Thank YOU, SIR. Spring came early this year. The citrus. Messed me up. But that's behind me now. I feel great."

"How soon can you get a room?"

Right to the point, I liked this guy more and more. I also liked HIS voice. That was important to me. If I was going to bottom for a guy he had to sound like a man.

"This week is Mother's Day. I want to be able to call back East on Sunday without sounding beaten up. But next week would work fine."

"OK. That works for me. I can come out on Saturday after work. I'll e-mail you this week with instructions. It's late now. I need to get back to work. Look for me online. That's an order."

"Yes, SIR." With that HE hung up.

The next day I put in my reservation at my roommate's resort, making sure I got my favorite room. The one in the corner with some privacy and a view of the mountain. It was available and my name went in the book.

The adrenaline of this possible encounter stayed with me. During my work out that day I felt stronger. My fears of re-injury had slowly dissipated as I progressed in the new training routine and my confidence grew. I upped the weight for a few of the exercises. It helped to have some more motivation.

I was sore and tired when the workout was finished but it felt thrilling to be pushing my body. Once home I made myself a protein drink and ate a big protein lunch. I loved having the gym be such an important part of my life again and it was so convenient to live just a few minutes from it. Back up in Sonoma County it took forty-five minutes just to drive to the Gold's Gym in Santa Rosa.

Sunday afternoon is a fun time at the Barracks Bar. With the weather warm, the shirts would be off. After a few months of good workouts, I was ready to expose my upper body with a cocky confidence. Other than having to hold in my stomach, it was good to feel sure about myself. Whether I met someone or not, didn't matter. It was a time to be seen. Now that I'd been going to World Gym, I started to recognize more people. Regardless, an hour or so is about all I could take and the time went by fast. It was a nice even combination of acquaintances and cruise time. I left with a sense of a major accomplishment, alone, but not lonely.

"This is SIR," the message read. "Did you get the room?"

"Yes SIR," I wrote back. "Got it for Saturday and Sunday night."

"Excellent," read HIS reaction the following day. "Here are your first instructions. Write them down so you don't forget them or lose them. From now on you are to end all your e-mails to SIR with the words SIR's subhole. Is that understood?"

No one had had ever given me a name before. I'd been called plenty of names because of the things I had written in my column and had said and done in my political activism. I replied to his instructions, "Yes SIR. Understood, subhole."

The next night the phone rang. "Did you read the e-mail I sent you telling you how I want you to respond?" That deep seductive voice spoke into my ear.

My body tensed. I read it and had followed it precisely. "Yes SIR. I did."

"Read the email again. Out loud." His voice tightened. Irritated.

I quickly pulled up the web site, happy that my roommate had convinced me to get Road Runner cable internet connection, which kept the phone lines free. "From now on you are to end all e-mails to SIR with the words SIR's subhole."

"How did you end your message to SIR?" Now HE sounded stern.

"subhole." Shit, HE was right I hadn't followed precisely. I'd already made a mistake. There was silence. How did I miss that? I was unsure what to say now and growing more uncomfortable with the silence. "So YOU want me to actually write 'SIR's subhole?'"

"That's what it says."

SIR's subhole implied ownership and possession. Stunned. It felt like I'd walked into an unseen glass wall. And titillated, too. I'd never been owned by anyone. Oh, sure a couple of them acted like I was their possession. But signing it this way meant my acceptance of the arrangement. My consent. "Sorry SIR. I just didn't think YOU wanted both words. I'd never done this before. I can do this." I had made my first giant leap into the unknown.

"It's pretty easy. Just follow MY instructions precisely." HIS voice sounded confident.

I felt embarrassed. This guy is going to think I'm stupid, I thought. I'd made a stupid mistake. It was simple. "Yes SIR. Sorry. I got it."

"I hope you do. I'll be sending more instructions. Make sure you follow them clearly. It's late tonight. Good night, subhole."

"Good night SIR." I hung up the phone and sat back. Wow! This guy is something else. HE's for real. This is exactly what I wanted. I pulled up HIS pic hoping to find some clue as to what HE was really like. This time there was a second picture. HE looked slender and muscular. I hoped HE was beefy. Under the category Body Hair HE wrote – some. It looked like HE had more than some. I hoped HE was hairy. More hair the better. That would be perfect. Hairy and muscular. HE was clean shaven and handsome with a broad face exactly the kind that I liked. I preferred beards and goatees. But this was changing. The hairy chest and handsome were the keys. They can always grow a beard. You can't grow a hairy chest. You gotta have one first.

Now it was time to let HIM know some things about me so I wrote. "You should know that I'm hard of hearing. I wear hearing aids. I'm not deaf. I can hear on the phone because I use an amplified phone. Just letting you know ahead of time so there are no surprises."

The next day I read this message "When you're with SIR there are only three things that I want to hear out of your mouth. Make sure you write them down and remember them. Number 1 –

Yes SIR. Number 2 – Thank YOU SIR. Number three – subhole's only purpose is to serve the SIR. I want you to practice saying them to yourself."

When I read this I thought to myself – those are the only things I can say? How is that going to happen?

The phone rang the next night. "It's SIR. Did you get your instructions?"

"Yes SIR."

"Good. Repeat what I told you."

"The only things I'm to say is 'Yes SIR,' 'Thank You SIR,' 'subhole's only purpose is to serve the SIR.'"

"That's right. Have you been repeating it so you know it when I ask?"

"Yes SIR."

"I hope so. You'll be punished if you don't remember."

"Yes SIR. I understand."

"Now get a piece of paper and write down these things that we're going to need."

I found a pad of paper and pulled out a pen. "I have it SIR."

"SIR likes Gatorade to drink. Get some bottles of Gatorade for SIR. A couple of aromatic candles, and water to drink."

I wrote down the word Gatorade. "What kind of Gatorade SIR?"

"SIR likes Orange Gatorade."

"Orange Gatorade. Yes SIR." I added it.

"A cigar for SIR."

"Yes SIR. Any particular kind?"

"Pick one out. Ask at the shop. A mild one."

"Yes SIR. I'll do that." I wondered what HE was doing at the other end. How HE was dressed? Where HE was sitting?

"Get a couple of bottles of Bactine. The spray bottle. You've used that before, haven't you?"

"I think so SIR. It's an antiseptic spray."

"That's right. Also get a couple of bottles of Noxzema. You know what that is, don't you?"

"I think so SIR. The white creamy stuff."

"That's it. I want you to report back to me as you get each item. Is that understood?"

"Yes SIR. I can do that."

"Don't forget the scented candles."

"Yes SIR."

"I'm not going to be able to get out there until Saturday night."

"Yes SIR. That's fine. SIR, how much time are you planning to spend with me?"

"That's a strange question. You looking to play with other guys, too?"

"No SIR. Just want to know what you're thinking."

"I'm planning to stay in your room for the night, if it works out. Is that alright?"

"Yes SIR. It is. That would be nice."

Then SIR hung up. Seemed like a normal question to me. Always like to know what is expected ahead of time. Don't usually like guys staying over at my house. But since we'd be at the resort the pressure would be less. Wouldn't have to clean the house. Wouldn't have to get up and make breakfast. The resort offers coffee and tea, some cereal and English muffins and bagels. A good array of choices. Worse came to worse we could go out for breakfast.

The upcoming sexual scene with SIR gave me new motivation to workout. I wanted to look my best. Not that I really needed any extra focus. My workouts were for me and I was determined to make up for all those years of living in fear. Doing just two sets and hoping I wouldn't get sick. Now I was pushing my body hard again. Four, five, sometimes six sets. Pushing my muscles to exhaustion. Trusting that they would recover and bounce back after appropriate rest. It was truly gratifying. Hiring a trainer was such a smart decision. Each time I looked in the mirror and liked what I saw reinforced my conviction that I wasn't going to get sick. Each pound I gained was a pound towards the living and a step from the grim reaper. But our impending session did help me push the weights around with a little more determination. When I stepped on the scale that day it read 179. I would be 180 when I met SIR.

Over the next few days, I gathered the requested items. The first stop was Rite Aid for Noxzema and Bactine. I actually had butterflies in my stomach entering the store. No one had ever given me orders like this before. I always wanted someone to. No. That's not true. In actuality, I liked it when they did the work. Now that I had my chance I didn't want to mess it up. It seemed easy enough. But I always find a way to screw it up. Today, I walked up and down the aisles looking for the products. My eyes searched for a blue container. So many products. All slightly different. Finally I stood in front of the blue Noxzema product. It came in different sizes and containers. Why couldn't there be just one choice, I thought? Do I get the jar that you apply with you hand? Or will SIR prefer the kind that pumps out. Then how much should I buy? What size containers should I get?

After several minutes playing out the scenario in my mind about how each product might be used I was able to narrow my options. The pump jars of Noxzema were probably the best choice. You don't have to worry about losing the cap or getting the contents dirty. At the risk of running out, I bought four of them.

With one task accomplished and somewhat relieved, I moved onto the next item. I finally found the Bactine in a white container with green lettering and a red dot on the front. Now the same choices. What kind of container? What size container? Each time I'm presented with options like this I flash back to the movie Unbearable Lightness of Being. About two people from Eastern Europe, before the wall came down, who make it to the West and find it's too hard with too many decisions.

For me, it's always fear of making a mistake especially in this case, with someone new. I didn't want HIM to think I couldn't follow instructions. I was fearful a mistake would happen in the middle of our scene and HE'd be upset.

As I purchased each item I crossed it off the list. The water was easy. The Gatorade was easy. How much should I buy? What if we ran out? These are things I would normally fret about as a host anyway. Buying for HIM added a slightly higher level of anxiety. Should I get a different flavor just to be sure? To please HIM. To be ready and anticipate HIS needs. I wanted HIM to like me.

That night the phone rang. There was a twinge in my belly.

"How are you doing with that list I gave you?" a deep voice said.

I hoped it was HIM. "Getting through it pretty well, SIR. Just have the cigar to get."

"Good subhole. SIR is pleased."

"Thank YOU, SIR." I said slightly giddy. I hoped HE wouldn't notice my nervousness. If HE did, HE never mentioned it.

"You sure you got the room?" HE reiterated.

"Yes SIR, I phoned over there today to double check. Everything is ready."

"SIR is planning on arriving around 10:30. What time can you get the room?"

"I'm gonna start bringing things over there around noon, SIR. Would it please YOU for me to work out on Saturday?"

"No, skip Saturday. I want you rested and in top condition to take as much abuse as I wish to give. I don't want any sore muscles or injuries or excuses. Is that understood?"

"Yes, SIR."

"I'll leave if you don't behave and follow MY orders."

"Yes, understood."

"What's your cell phone number?"

"Um, I don't have a cell phone SIR."

"You don't have a cell phone?"

I could hear the judgment. What kind of person doesn't have a cell phone, HE must be thinking. "There wasn't phone service where I lived before, SIR. I never needed one." I hoped HE would understand.

"Is there a phone in the room? How am I going to get a hold of you?"

"There's a phone in the room. We're in room 40. That's the room I always get. The front office can transfer YOU."

"I guess that's how it'll have to be, I can't believe you don't have a cell phone. Anyway, SIR will check in with you tomorrow. Dismissed."

"SIR, there's one more thing."

"What's that subhole?" I could hear some exasperation.

"I have a dog, SIR."

"What kind of dog?"

"A Golden Retriever, SIR."

"Can someone watch him?"

"I don't have anyone who can do that. I don't know many people here, yet, SIR."

"What do you usually do with him?"

"He comes with me, SIR. Dogs are allowed at the resort. He can stay outside while we play. He always does that."

"Can't he stay at your house?"

"He could, but then I'd have to go and walk him early in the morning."

"You don't have a doggie door?"

"No, SIR. It was blocked over when they closed in the porch."

"He's not going to bark and try to bite when I string you up and beat you?"

"No, SIR. Russell just likes to watch. We can put him out when we do that."

"I don't like this. But it'll have to be, I guess. Try to find someone to take him. It'll just be better for everyone."

"Yes, SIR. I will."

"Dismissed."

"Yes SIR. Thank YOU SIR."

HE hung up. This last part of our conversation troubled me. My dog is a vital part of my life. I hoped that SIR came to understand this.

CHAPTER THREE

Preparation

Since it was off season in Palm Springs the room was vacant, enabling me to get the keys early on Saturday. Since I had never set up an S&M scene I was a bit apprehensive and eager to start. The first thing needed done was to rearrange the furniture. Currently, the Queen size bed sat in the middle of the room. This is fine if you're hanging a sling, as is usually the case at The Camp, and what is more in line with my experience also. Then the bed isn't an obstacle as the hooks are on the left side giving plenty of access to the exposed hole. But for this arrangement, there needs to be complete access around a body strung up to the hooks, my strung up body.

The bed had to go. This meant moving it to the far side of the room. Luckily the bed frame had wheels and it moved easily. There was just enough room to drag the desk situated by the front door over to the window, creating a large unimpeded space in front of the hooked up area. Putting the night stands into the small kitchen gave ample room from behind. This set-up allowed a person to use a flogger or similar items, to aim appropriately to the desired body parts without hitting other unintended things like lamps or mirrors.

For a moment, I envisioned SIR in the room, moving around, imagining what HE might want to do. What might please HIM? No other arrangement seemed better. I hoped HE'd be pleased.

As morning turned to afternoon I returned home and got the coolers out of the backyard storage shed and cleaned out the dust. Each room at the resort has a small fridge, not nearly large enough for drinks and food for two days for two people. I would need the coolers to keep things cold and safe. Next on the list was what to wear even though I expected to be naked most of the time. I anticipated all the different scenarios that might demand an outfit: breakfast at Bit of Country, coffee at Koffi, a walk through Ruth Hardy Park or the Las Palmas neighborhood, a drive around Warm Sands, Sunday beer bust at The Barracks. I wanted to be ready for all the possibilities. And you never knew what condition the clothes might end up in.

Just in case we somehow ended up back at my house it was important that it looked a bit clean. Since I'm not a neat and tidy guy this would have been a huge endeavor and not one I was about to take on. I figured as long as the kitchen sink looked cleaned it would pass an initial inspection. And if my bedroom looked kept I wouldn't hear too many comments. Everything else I could blame on the roommate.

It was time to make another trip back over to the resort. Shortly after two the hotel room phone rang. "Hello."

"Hello subhole, you getting everything done?"

"Hello, SIR. Yes SIR. I got the room ready already."

"You got the room ready? Good work. What's it look like?"

"I connected the chains to the hooks and strung them across the ceiling to the hook on the other side. I got the bed in the corner of the room, out of the way."

"Sounds good. Can't wait to see it. I want you to lay out all the equipment on the bed for SIR."

"Yes SIR."

"I'm still not going to get out of here until around 8 o'clock tonight. How long does it take to get there?"

"Depends on the traffic, SIR. At least two hours."

"So that gets me there at 10.

"Yes, SIR."

"How am I going to get into the resort?"

"I'll tell them I'm expecting someone. I'll leave your name at the front desk."

"Are you sure that will be enough? I want you in a jock strap, on your knees when I arrive."

"Yes, SIR."

"Tell me how I want to find you."

"In my jock strap and on my knees when you arrive."

"That's right. You're going to get punished if I find you any other way."

"Yes SIR."

"Do they have videos?"

"Yes SIR."

"Pick out a video. I want a video playing with the sound off. Do you have any music?"

"Some, SIR.

"Get a CD player for the room. I want the music playing and the video sound off."

"Yes SIR."

"How am I going to get a hold of you this evening? I want to call you when I'm leaving LA."

"There's a phone in the room. The front desk will transfer the call."

"I can't believe you don't have a cell phone."

I didn't respond. It's difficult for some people to understand. I hate cell phones.

"It better go through. I don't want any hitches. Is that understood?"

"Yes SIR."

"Dismissed, I'll call before I leave." The phone call ended. Conversations with HIM always got my pulse racing and my stomach twitching.

Rather than use the ice machine at the resort I drove over to Stater Brothers to buy a couple of bags of ice for the coolers. It's only a few blocks to the resort so there's no chance to melt, even in the heat. I set the coolers down in the small kitchen–like area, out of the way, and got an ample amount of each of the drinks iced, storing the rest under the counter where they could be easily retrieved.

Though there was plenty of time before SIR's arrival, each section of chores completed was a huge relief. Setting the toys out on the bed was an easy task. I put the floggers together, the blindfolds together, the handcuffs and restraints together. This gave me a chance to take inventory to make sure everything was there: jock strap, boots, chaps and leather vest.

In the back of my mind I couldn't help think that SIR might try to trick me and suddenly announce an early arrival, sending me scurrying around frantically to get everything ready. I liked to prepare slowly and methodically and was never one to crash study or pull an all-nighter in school.

Next came getting my clothes out of the duffle bag and into the drawers or hung in the closet. I left plenty of room for SIR to hang any clothes HE might bring. Also, leaving plenty of room in the drawers for HIM, too.

Finally the clock ticked past 6 pm. Just a few more hours to go. The final task for me to do before closing down the house for the evening was to take Russell to the dog park for an hour. Fortunately there were enough other dogs and their owners to give him lots of opportunities to run, sniff and get attention. Though it concerned me that he didn't get his business done. The hour passed quickly.

I stopped by the house one last time just to make sure there wasn't anything I forgot, because there always was. I checked off all the items in my brain one more time. The food, drinks, clothes, toys, Russell's food and dishes. Like I said, I'm the kind of guy who anticipated any scenario and then spent forever preparing for them and at some point, usually when I'm at the brink of exhaustion, finally stops. Well, not today. This was it and it felt good to close the door. No more errands. The move-over completed.

The phone in Room 40 rang shortly after eight pm. "Everything ready for SIR, subhole?"

"Yes SIR. I'm here in the room. Everything is ready."

"You in your jock strap?"

"No SIR. Not yet."

"Well, where is it?"

"Right here on the bed, SIR. Just waiting a little bit to put it on. Still need to go down and get a video."

"Put it on, right now."

"Now?"

"Yes, NOW. While I'm on the phone."

"Yes SIR." I grabbed the jock strap and slid one leg through it, then the other. "It's on SIR."

"How's it feel?"

"A little tight."

"Good. Now leave it on."

"Yes SIR."

"SIR is leaving LA now. I'll be there in two hours. SIR is looking forward to using HIS subhole."

"Thank YOU, SIR."

"What's that exit I take in to Palm Springs?"

"111, SIR."

"111. How far away is the place from there?"

"Another fifteen or twenty minutes, SIR."

"Fine, I'll call when I get on 111. When I call I want you to get on your knees and stay on your knees and think about serving your SIR. Is that understood?"

"Yes SIR."

"Tell me what you're going to do."

"YOU're going to call when you get on 111. I'm going to get on my knees and stay there and think about serving my SIR."

"Exactly. Dismissed."

Two hours can seem like an eternity. I slipped on my shorts and used the time to go down to the office to pick out a video. Not being a big fan of porn, I'd rather do it than watch it; I wasn't sure what to pick out. The resort specialized in fucking and butt play, not SM. Also, not knowing SIR, I really wasn't sure what kind of guys HE was into. If HE liked me it must be smooth muscle guys. Just to be safe I chose a couple of different ones. When I got back to the room, the hands of the clock didn't seem like they had moved forward much while I was completing that chore. I didn't really know what to do with myself. Since May is already hot in the desert, I used the extra time to relax and cool off in the pool. This also gave me a chance to show the dog some last minute attention. I threw his ball from one end of the pool to the other end of the resort. He raced down the side, exuberantly jumping over several lounge chairs and retrieved it. Normally he wouldn't be able to play like this at a resort but having lived with the owner for many years in San Francisco, besides getting a free room, gave extra benefits to the dog, too.

I admit I was nervous and apprehensive, worrying how I would perform; wondering if HE'd like me; if HE'd be pleased with the room. So playing with the dog was good activity for me. I lobbed it over the pool a few times before moving into the jacuzzi. The warm water relaxed the nervousness I felt.

An hour had lapsed much to my relief. Soon HE would be calling. There were still some things I could do. The videos needed to be checked because all too often they're damaged and the guests just turn them in. After all this effort I didn't want to discover this too late and the instructions were to have the volume off and the music on. That could take a few tries to get it right. It was also wise to check the remote since often times they didn't work properly, either. Batteries could wear out or any number of things could go wrong.

And it's a good thing I checked, because, of course, the remote wasn't working properly. After several attempts on my own to get it functioning it was necessary to phone the front office. The boy came up and knew exactly what to do.

Then the phone rang. "Are you on your knees?"

"Yes SIR. I am."

"Is everything ready?"

"It's all set SIR."

"SIR is getting off of highway 10 at the Palm Springs exit. How much longer from here?"

"About twenty minutes, SIR."

"Are you sure my name is at the front desk?"

"Yes, SIR. I checked again."

"There better not be any problems."

I thought to myself, I hope there aren't any problems. One of the drawbacks of having a resort owner as a friend and using those prerogatives was occasionally someone on the staff took their resentments out on me. There could always be a minor problem. It was usually a pissy kind of thing. Nothing serious. I hoped this time things would go smooth.

"Ring the buzzer in the front and someone will let YOU in. The office is to the right. Just give them your name. Ask 'em to show YOU where room 40 is."

SIR hung up.

The phone rang again. "Russell just went on the grass. Please come down and pick it up."

"Ohh, Russell," I mumbled to myself. In a split second decision I knew the office boy would continue to harass me until I picked it up. He was the worst one with the pissy things. I threw on my shorts and hoped SIR would be late.

I rushed out the door and closed it behind me, instantly knowing I had made a bigger blunder. First things first. It was only a short distance down to the front of the resort. From experience I knew the places Russell used. I grabbed a plastic bag and scooped up the debris and disposed of it properly.

Then I walked into the office. "All picked up. Now I need the master key. I locked myself out."

He made a scowling face that I learned to ignore, as he got up from his chair and handed me the keys. I turned and quickly moved towards my room, knowing that time was short. I opened the door, unlocked it and made sure I didn't make the same mistake again. I rushed back down to the office where the boy was smoking a cigarette outside and I handed him the keys.

Just then a tall man appeared from around the wall of hedges. HE was clean shaven and handsome and more handsome than HIS picture. HE looked like HE'd gained a little weight, too. I liked that.

"Russell had an accident. I had to come down and take care of it and then I locked myself out." I said it hoping for some understanding. Hoping HE wouldn't turn around and leave, yet knowing I was in trouble.

HIS face tightened and HIS keen grey eyes got small. Definitely not a pleased look.

"The room's already. Everything's ready. I'm sorry. I'm really sorry. I was up there waiting for YOU. I was." This time I appealed for some mercy.

"I told you I wanted you in the room waiting," HE said in a low slow tense pissed-off voice.

I looked down towards the ground and shrugged my shoulders. In a softer voice I said, "I couldn't let this wait. I had no choice. I had to get it done."

"Go back up there and wait for ME. Where are the keys? You're going to be punished for disobeying ME."

There was nothing for me to say to change the situation. I handed HIM the keys, turned and rushed up to the room unsure of what would happen now. I closed the door to the room, got on my knees and waited. I listened for footsteps on the walkway outside. I listened for the turn of the door knob; any evidence that HE was there. I tried to calculate how long it took to go from the front of the resort, drive around the block to the guest parking lot in the back, unload a car and carry things up to the second level to room 40.

My breathing became shallow as some panic set in. Waiting made me anxious. Waiting made me insecure. So many times people say they're coming over and don't show up. Where was HE?

It seemed like a long time had passed. What was HE doing? What did HE think of me? What was HE going to do to me?

I heard the door pushed open. HE was here. The anxiousness turned to apprehension. I kept my head low and averted eye contact. If I hadn't already seen HIM the impulse may have been too strong. Still, out of the corner of my eye I saw that HE brought HIS duffle bag into the room and walked to the back. HE moved with such certainty, as though he were already familiar with the room. HE had this aura about HIM. Of course, I was projecting but it felt so natural. I was already HIS.

HE sat down on the chair I placed for HIM in the middle of the room. "Put your head on my lap."

"I'm so sorry. I'm sorry. Please don't be angry with me."

HE grabbed my head. "Don't speak unless spoken to. What have I been teaching you to say this last week? What are the only things I want to you to say?" HE leaned forward.

"Yes, SIR. Thank YOU, SIR. It's only purpose is the serve the SIR," I said loudly.

"That's right. That's all I want to hear from you. Nothing else. And you don't have to shout it into my ear. You'll be punished if you say anything else. Is that understood?"

"Yes, SIR," I said in a loud voice.

HE let go of my head and I lowered my face.

"What's its only purpose tonight?"

I leaned up and shouted. "Its only purpose is to serve the SIR."

"You don't have to shout," HE said. "Just say it in a regular voice. I'm not the one who is deaf. Let's try it again. What's subhole's only purpose?"

"Its only purpose is to serve the SIR," I said it in a calm lowered voice."

SIR patted my head. "That was much better. That's how I want it said."

"Yes SIR." I looked down towards the floor.

"Stick your ass out. I want to see it."

I lengthened my body out in yoga like position and stuck my ass high in the air.

"More."

I stretched further.

SMACK! HIS hand slapped the crack of my ass hard.

"Oogh." It stung and the sensation spread across both cheeks. Then there was stillness.

"What do you say?" HE demanded, in a low voice.

"Thank YOU, SIR."

"What took you so long?" Another strike. This time sharper and it stung more.

"Thank YOU, SIR."

"That's better. Now get down there and lick my boots."

I lunged at his boots and ran my tongue along the black leather. I'd only ever done this once before. I enjoyed it then but planting my tongue on a guy's boots isn't the first thing I normally think about doing to a hot man. I'm usually a right-for-the-cock kind of guy. Tonight I found this service tantalizing.

"Slower." Another stinging hand spank across my ass.

"Oh yeah," I mumbled, breathlessly. "Thank YOU, SIR."

"Slow. Like you mean it. Not like some crazy person."

"Yes SIR. Sorry SIR."

I took a deep breath and calmly licked the front, then moved onto the back side of the boot.

"What do you say?"

"Thank You SIR."

HE cuffed my ass roughly again. "I shouldn't have to ask you, subhole?" HE withdrew this boot and pushed out the left one.

"Thank You SIR."

"That's better."

Slower, much slower, my tongue glided along the right side of the toe. "Thank You SIR." I skimmed back along to the left side and my cock throbbed. "THANK YOU SIR!" I shifted my body to reach behind.

"Lean up."

Responding quickly, I bent back up on my knees.

HE backhanded my stomach. "Hold in your stomach."

I sucked in my belly.

"Hold your shoulders back." HIS voice was firm.

I obeyed.

"Hold your head high."

Now I felt exposed.

"Never look directly at ME. Hold your head high but keep your eyes looking down unless I say so. Understand?"

"Yes SIR. Thank YOU SIR." I looked down towards the ground but could still see HIM pull HIS pants down a bit.

"Now lick my balls."

"Thank YOU SIR." I leaned forward and licked his big hairy balls. They tasted salty from sweat with a pungent odor. This action was more my comfort level. "Thank YOU SIR." I licked under the ball sac, conscious about being hasty. There was something exhilarating about going slow. I often rushed into my sex acts quickly and forcefully. Going slow usually made my dick soft. There was no soft dick tonight. In fact I knew it was dripping.

CHAPTER FOUR

The Training Begins

"Now lick my cock." HE spoke calmly with a deep commanding voice.

"Thank YOU SIR." It was odd to follow orders about something like this. But I liked the change. I had never really let anyone else control me this way. Unhurriedly, I slid my tongue along HIS cock, marking each spot. It was a good size, thick, and probably just under eight inches. I had to temper my desire to immediately take it in my mouth. I suspected HE didn't want that, yet. My tongue slithered up to the mushroom head and wet the tip then ran down the underside to the base.

"Now open your mouth, subhole, and suck it slowly."

I felt I had just won the lottery. Eureka is what I wanted to shout just before HIS cock got devoured. It was wide but not too wide that my teeth were a concern.

"Lick the head and then suck it," SIR said.

Eagerly my tongue was on the swollen head and I opened my mouth wide to take it deep down my throat. I pulled away and followed through again. I heard HIM moan as HIS sex tool inched towards the recesses of my throat. I had a strong desire to go faster to please HIM more, and myself, but resisted, believing that would displease HIM and might make HIM stop. So I continued paying attention to a slow pace.

"Sit up and lean back."

I followed HIS order.

SIR stood.

"Now take off MY boots."

I leaned forward and untied the lacings of HIS right boot. They were low rise so it wasn't too difficult. I was relieved they weren't the kind that rose up to the calves. It usually took so much effort to get them off that I lost the craving. SIR's boot pulled off easily, exposing HIS wide foot. "Thank YOU SIR." I moved towards the second one and off it came. "Thank YOU SIR."

"Get down there and smell MY socks."

The grey socks were of thick cotton. They were musty and smelled like an old jock strap. A dog would enjoy running with these.

"Now take off MY pants."

I pulled at the waist of HIS black athletic sweat pants and they slipped down easily. One at time, I lifted HIS legs and pulled the pants under HIS feet then folded them neatly, placing them on the bed behind me.

SIR sat back down and raised HIS leg. "Now the socks."

"Thank you SIR." I pulled one sock at a time down around HIS ankles and off HIS feet.

"Lick them."

I stared at HIS thick wide smooth-skinned foot for a moment and softly said, "Thank YOU SIR."

I had never done this to any one's foot before. The opportunity never presented itself. I tongued the top of HIS foot and slid around, slowly. This was good; I thought, then took the plunge and glided along the tops of HIS toes. "Thank You SIR." I licked one toe at a time then lifted HIS foot and took the baby toe into my mouth. Then the second one. I could feel my breathing quicken and my cock throbbing beneath me. Slow, I thought, slow, and moved to the third one and sucked on it as if it was a cock. Then shifted to the fourth one and finally the big toe. I attempted to put all five toes into my mouth at once, eventually getting them in. After this I switched to the bottom of HIS foot, starting at the ridge and progressing down to the heel. "Thank You SIR."

"Now subhole, lick your way up my body. And do it slow and don't miss a spot."

"YES SIR. Thank YOU SIR." Slowly, placing my tongue on his right foot I glided along the instep towards SIR's hairy shin. I aimed sideways around the lower wide calf sliding up the thick muscle. "Thank YOU, SIR." Then I shifted to the inner side continuing up SIR's calf, centering at the knee. My tongue licked the knee cap and slowly investigated the hidden darker back side. It tasted salty. It was exciting to be servicing a man like this and stimulating to be providing pleasure to another guy without expecting any reciprocation.

I travelled between HIS legs to the inner side again. HIS cock was hard and I had a clear path to it but I knew that wasn't what SIR wanted. I resisted my usual desire and slowly licked SIR's thick hairy inner thigh. HIS legs were like tree stumps and turned me on. Most guys that work out forget their legs and they look like toothpicks dangling below their broad upper bodies. Like chicken legs. I spent a few minutes at HIS thigh, running my tongue up and down, from side to side. My pulse quickened. It took a lot of resistance not to lunge at HIS long erect cock. Seeing SIR's erection erased from my mind any thought that HE might be getting bored. I readjusted my body to have access to HIS outer thigh. "Thank YOU, SIR."

As much as I enjoyed SIR's muscular legs I was eager to proceed north to taste and feel HIS hairy stomach. One of my favorite parts of a man's body.

With SIR sitting, I maneuvered between HIS legs and started on one side just above HIS hip. Hair was everywhere. I slowly licked HIS stomach like a cat laps a bowl of milk feeling the bristles against my tongue. My pulse quickened again. I took several longer brush strokes along HIS solid stomach and decided to do something I truly enjoyed but rarely did. I thought HE might disapprove but decided it was worth the possible punishment and if I asked permission HE might not let me. So, bringing my tongue back in my mouth, I buried my face into HIS stomach, submerging it into HIS muscular furry abdomen and rubbing it from side to side feeling the strands bristling against my skin. Ecstasy. Pure ecstasy, and gratefully, there was no repercussion. When I thought I'd paused long enough for my own pleasure, I continued up, shifting higher past HIS navel and slowly following the under cleavage of HIS pec muscles. In my excitement, my initial response was to bite into HIS nipples but I sensed this wasn't how to play so I carefully massaged the left one. Then with some confidence, lightly flicked at the tip. "Thank YOU, SIR."

I journeyed over to the second one and along the upper ridge of HIS big pecs. Hair still covered HIS body.

Then SIR lifted one arm. "Go slow and show ME you mean it."

"Thank YOU, SIR." My impulse said to rush so I took a slow breath and moved my face close and inhaled. No cologne smell was a relief and I took my first small lick. Next, I took a deep stroke with my tongue along the lower half of the pit. Then moved to the center and drew a straight line up and down finally rubbing my face in HIS moist pit absorbing HIS smell. "Thank YOU, SIR," I growled, a happy subhole.

HE lifted the opposite arm.

"Thank YOU, SIR." I swung to the other side. First I tasted it, and then spread my tongue around. HE smelled so good I couldn't help not rubbing my face all around. "Thank YOU, SIR."

Then SIR held his left arm out and flexed HIS bicep. It was only then that I could make out the chain link tattoo circling it. I licked HIS bulked up muscle, running my tongue along the black and blue links. Man, I loved HIS big hairy body.

SIR stood up. "Lean up." He walked over to the bed and reviewed the arranged equipment. HE picked up the wrist restraints and returned to where I knelt. "Let me see your hands."

I obeyed.

SIR placed the first restraint on my wrist, tugging it a couple of times to get it snug. The tightness was exhilarating.

"Thank You, SIR."

The second restraint went on quicker. SIR clipped them behind my back.

"Thank You, SIR."

HE sat back in HIS chair and examined HIS possession. "Lift your shoulders up subhole."

I obeyed.

"Pull your stomach in." SIR slapped HIS hand across my right pec muscle. It stung sharply and I grunted a bit.

"What do you say, subhole?"

"Thank YOU SIR."

"You better thank ME. Taking the time to correct your posture. I don't want a slouching slave."

"Yes SIR."

HIS hand slapped the other pec muscle.

"Thank YOU SIR."

He twisted each erect nipple with two fingers.

"Thank YOU SIR."

Then HE sat back. "Now get down here and show ME how happy you are to serve MY cock."

I positioned myself to maintain my balance. We forget how much we use our hands and shoulders to keep steady. I opened my mouth wide and slowly sucked HIS sexmeat, taking special care not to list to one side and scrape it. I took my time and calmly sucked the head, gently moving further down the shaft to the base. I was able to take HIS whole cock without gagging. It took some stomach muscle control to enable me to withdraw without going off kilter.

"Lean back." SIR stood and unclipped the restraints. "Come over here." SIR reached for a second hook and clipped one restraint to the bolt in the ceiling. "That comfortable?"

"YES SIR, Thank YOU SIR."

HE clipped the other restraint to the opposite side, facing me into the room.

"Thank YOU, SIR." It had been a long time since I found myself in this position. Probably ten years or more since I let any one place me into this vulnerable stance. It was dangerous to let a stranger do this. But it was a chance I was willing to take. Especially at the resort where people were around and the office boy did see HIM.

SIR walked over to HIS toy bag and pulled out a riding crop. I remembered enough to know that this could be painful and that the key was to breathe. Fear was the enemy and at the moment there was some fear. Breathing calmed me.

SIR glided the tip of the black leather riding crop along my smooth chest and down my stomach. HE flipped it against my right pec.

"Ohh." I took a deep breath.

"What do you say, subhole?"

"Thank YOU SIR."

"Took you long enough."

"YES SIR."

"IF I'm going to take the time to give you what you want I expect you to be a grateful subhole. Are you grateful subhole?"

"Yes SIR."

The crop struck the other pec, slightly harder.

"Oohh. Thank YOU, SIR." I hoped I could handle HIM.

"That's better, subhole." The crop smacked against my stomach.

"Thank YOU, SIR." This was it, I thought. No turning back now.

The next one hit my inner thigh.

"Ouh. Thank YOU SIR."

SIR stepped back to the bed where the accessories lay, searching among the items. HE picked up a gag and stepped behind me. He placed the ball piece snug in my mouth and latched it in place. Then HE stood in front of me with the riding crop back in HIS hand and smacked it hard against my chest.

I cried out a mumbled reaction. The leather crop slapped against the other side. A moment later against my stomach. I took a deep breath, relaxed, and stood tall. I'd been waiting for this.

SIR tapped the insides of my thighs. "Spread your legs."

Now it's going to hurt, I thought, and took a deep breath. The crop tapped my balls and reflexively I jerked a bit. HE hit them again. "What do you say subhole?"

"Thank you SIR," I said in a muffled manner because I was holding my breath. I didn't know how it sounded to HIM.

The crop tapped the side of my enlarged cock a few times. This I liked. HE smacked my balls again with more force.

"Oouu." My body jerked to the side.

Again, harder.

My body rocked like in an earthquake.

"Breathe, subhole. Breathe."

I took a deep breath and the shaking slowed.

SIR turned back towards the bed as I watched HIM search among the items. HE picked up one of the blindfolds and stretched it out. HE put it back down and picked up a second one then walked to me and placed it over my eyes, taking a moment to adjust it.

Already without full hearing senses, I was now unable to see as well. My body shook from fear. I breathed deep and slowly, the shaking subsided. I stood calm, relaxed, prepared for the feel of the leather somewhere against my skin but jumped skittishly as the leather softly glided along my chest. Focusing on breathing, I closed my eyes.

Smack! It struck against my right pec muscle. Another one a moment later on the left pec. Then a sharp sting on the side of my stomach, followed by a matching one on the other side. "What do you say subhole?"

"Thank You SIR," I garbled.

There's another smack on the side of my stomach. "Ugh." I focused on breathing and not the stinging pain.

The crop slapped against the outside of my thigh quickly followed by one on the opposite side. My body tightened as I knew what was coming. I breathed and went deep inside just as the crop smacked against my balls. "Ugh." I moaned and instinctively jerked, but caught myself and returned to a still, upright position. The crop slapped against my balls again. "Oooh." It was a guttural groan with a mixture of pain and excitement. "Thank YOU SIR," I mumbled.

Several easy snaps hit my balls in a row. Without reacting, I focused on my breath. Slowly the intensity rose with each one quicker and harder. I willed myself to stay still and rose above the fear and pain. "Oohh." My breathing got shallow and it hurt.

A few smacked the head of my cock.

"Thank YOU SIR." The blows here didn't cause fear and my breathing returned to calm.

There was quiet and stillness. Then I sensed some movement. The leather slid gently across my upper back and I adjusted my point of reference. Again, taking several breaths was calming. The crop smacked the edge of the center of my back. A second strike hit the other side. The crop landed hard beneath my shoulder blade followed with a cross body matching blow. Then HE struck above my hip. Each belt a bit harder than before.

The crop smacked the outer area of my right cheek muscle hard. "Ugh. Thank YOU SIR." This at least was familiar territory. There's a similar hard crack to the other cheek.

"Stick your ass out, subhole."

I submitted.

Whack! Another hit the ass muscle. Then again on the opposite side. The smacks got harder. One after the other. Abruptly, the crop landed against the back of my thigh.

It stung and I cried out, "Oou."

Then HE hit the other side. SIR made HIS way systematically down both legs and slapped my calves. HE completed HIS marking of my body by reversing HIS trail. HE beat my ass, again, with several hard whacks and finishing off with a few more to the sides of my back.

The room went still.

"What do you say subhole?"

"Thank You, SIR," I whispered, coarsely.

I felt HIM near me. The blindfold came off. Then the gag. "Thank you, SIR."

I watched HIM reach up and unhook me. It felt good to have my arms free and down.

SIR sat on HIS chair. "Come over here subhole and get down in your position."

I knelt in front of HIM.

"Come here and put your face in my belly."

I wrapped my arms around HIS legs and rested my head on HIS hairy stomach and took comfort.

"Good work subhole. For your reward you get to suck MY cock some more. What do you say?"

"Thank YOU, SIR."

I took HIS cock into my mouth and sucked the head. Then I took it all the way down my throat and left it there for a bit. SIR's cock stiffened. I sucked up and down. Slowly, up and down. Sucking on the head and then down to the base.

"Back in position, subhole."

I obeyed.

"I think it's time to go down and take a jacuzzi. Where are those towels I told you to have ready?"

"On the shelf back there, SIR."

"Go get them. You got the key to the room?"

"Yes SIR."

"Don't lose it. I'm not going to forget what happened. You will be punished for that at some point."

I grabbed the towel and keys and put on my sandals. Maybe HE'd forget if I was good. "Would SIR like something to drink?"

"What do you got, subhole?"

"Gatorade, water, coke."

"Just some water."

"Yes SIR."

I grabbed a water out of the fridge then opened the door for SIR and followed HIM out.

Fortunately, there was no one else at the jacuzzi at this still relatively early Saturday night hour.

"Turn the jets on, subhole."

"Yes SIR. Thank you SIR."

The water was hot but not scalding. SIR got right in. It was still warm enough to me that I had to take my time and adjust.

SIR sat over in one of the curved-out ledges. "Come over here subhole and massage my neck."

I kneaded my fingers in to HIS thick and tight neck muscle.

"That's exactly it, subhole."

"Thank YOU, SIR." I pressed my fingers firmly into this area as SIR moaned and took deep breaths. Slowly I expanded the range to include SIR's neck and shoulders.

"Good work, subhole. That's enough for now. You have permission to sit over there." SIR pointed to the seat next to HIM.

"Thank YOU SIR." The hot water was relaxing to my shoulders and neck. Some spots on my body stung a bit but it was a good feeling, a used feeling, like working out at the gym.

"Will the owner get upset if someone uses an air mattress in here?"

"I don't know. I don't think so. Though I've never seen anyone use one in here before."

"Go get an air mattress for SIR."

I knew exactly where they were kept. "Yes SIR." I climbed the steps of the jacuzzi and walked over bare foot to the pool area. I choose one of the better rubber floats then returned and held it by the steps so SIR could lean back on to it without slipping off. The jets kept pushing the pad around in a circular motion so I had to hold it firmly in place. I'm surprised I had never seen anyone else do this before since the spa is enormous. Especially on some of the colder desert nights. Of course, how many have a slave to keep it in a position? I enjoyed holding it still for SIR but I actually found it more amusing than anything else. And it only worked because no other guests were there.

Holding the float steady I reached over and took his cock in my mouth, paying close attention not to scrape it with a tooth or to go too fast. This was for SIR's pleasure, not mine, and HIS hard cock was my reward. "Thank YOU, SIR."

Slowly, I took HIS cock further in, then back out and licked the head. Repeating the action again, deeper down my throat. Above the noise of the jacuzzi jets I heard HIM moan ever so slightly.

Amidst my own excitement, I worried that I might knock HIM off the float and displease HIM. I tempered my desires and focused on pleasing SIR.

Eventually the audacity of a float in a spa must have worn off. "That's enough subhole."

I navigated back over to the steps and SIR got off and stepped back into the water. "Which jet is the strongest?" HE asked.

"The one on the left is the strongest and the warmest, for some reason. I think because it's closest to the pump and heater."

SIR moved to that side of the jacuzzi.

"Come over here and rub my neck again, subhole."

I gladly obeyed and enjoyed touching SIR's hairy muscular body. We remained in there for a while longer. At that point a door to a nearby room opened and several men came and joined us. We greeted them but shortly returned to the privacy of our own dungeon. I immediately went down on my knees with my hands extended as SIR held the restraints. After buckling them firmly around my wrist HE hooked me to the ceiling.

"Thank YOU, SIR."

"What's your only purpose, subhole?"

"subhole's only purpose is the serve the SIR."

"That's right." SIR smacked the crop across my right pec.

"Thank YOU, SIR."

A smack against the other side.

"Thank YOU SIR."

HE slowly circled my body. The crop stung wherever it landed. My stomach. My thighs. My arms. My shoulder. My back. "Stick your ass out, subhole."

I leaned forward extending my ass up and out.

Whack!

"Thank YOU, SIR."

Smack!

"Thank YOU, SIR."

Again and again. My ass stung and warmed and I hoped HE would never stop. I heard some wrapper noise. A moment later, SIR moved close to me. HIS hands spread my ass checks apart and HE rammed HIS cock in.

"YES SIR! THANK YOU SIR!" I eagerly shouted, not expecting this.

He pounded faster and harder. Then slowed and moved it in and out. From behind me, SIR reached around and with both hands slugged my chest.

"Ugh." I could swear my body dropped four inches from the impact. "Thank YOU SIR," I said quieter, concealing my utter exhilaration.

HIS cock slid in and out several times. Again HIS fists pounded my chest. Once, twice, three times. Nothing could beat this.

"Thank YOU, SIR." I said, more steadily as the shock value dissipated. Nothing turned me on more than this.

Soon I heard SIR moaning loudly. I stuck my ass out further for HIM. HIS thrusts were forceful and long. I heard HIM cry out, "Fuck. Yeah. You fuckin' faggot. Cocksuckin' subhole faggot. Ohh. Yeah."

Then there was silence except for the music from the CD player that I suddenly heard along with SIR's heavy breathing. Shortly after, HIS cock slipped out and SIR sat in the chair still situated in the middle of the room. HE sat and looked at me admiringly, grin on HIS face.

I stood calmly, though now a bit self-conscious, wondering what would happen next. Soon, HE stood and walked over towards me and unclipped one arm and then the other. "I want to go back down to the jacuzzi. Get the things we need," HE said.

SIR walked out the door while I gathered up the towels, my sandals, the key and followed. As before the water felt good to my sore body. After a few minutes SIR said, "I want you to go back up to the room and get it ready to sleep. I want everything away except stuff to take a jacuzzi later. I'll be back up there soon. You wait for ME at the side of the bed."

I followed SIR's orders putting the equipment back into the suitcase and the chains into the box. It had been quite a night I thought as I put things away. HE was definitely the one for me I determined as I awaited HIS return on my knees at the side of the bed.

"Good work," HE said when HE opened the door and saw the room cleared.

"Now get in bed and turn to the right. You just lay there and go to sleep."

That would be the hardest thing I had done all night, I thought to myself, as I climbed in bed and turned right.

"Do they serve food at this place in the morning?"

"Coffee, some muffins and cereal."

"SIR would like some coffee in the morning. Two sugars and cream. Do you drink coffee?"

"No SIR. Tea."

"No cell phone and no coffee?" HE chuckled.

"And a dog," I couldn't help add.

HE laughed heartily and shook HIS head. "And a dog. Where is the dog?"

"Sitting outside the door."

"You have permission to bring him in."

"Thank you, SIR." HIS gesture eased my worries about having a dog around HIM. I opened the door and Russell rushed to SIR's side of the bed and lay down immediately.

"Good boy," SIR said.

At first it was difficult to sleep with HIM in the bed. I could feel HIS presence. Sometimes our bodies skimmed one another and I found myself wide awake again. But eventually sleep overcame me.

CHAPTER FIVE

Separation Meltdown

The next morning I awoke to an empty bed and no dog. I panicked at first but then saw SIR's belongings still there. The clock on the DVD player read 7am. I got out of bed and put on some shorts and sandals. I found the two of them in the jacuzzi. Well, not the dog, he was sitting by the jacuzzi.

"Would SIR like HIS coffee now?"

"Good idea, subhole. Did you sleep well?"

"Yes SIR. Did you?"

"Well enough," HE said.

I walked toward the back lobby where breakfast was served and returned with HIS coffee.

"I have breakfast plans with a friend at 9. I'll be back after. SIR would enjoy staying here till later this afternoon. Can subhole arrange for this?"

"Yes SIR. Happy to make that happen," I said with a wide smile.

SIR stepped up the jacuzzi stairs. I grabbed the towel and dried HIM off.

"What are you going to do while I'm at breakfast?"

"I can have a bowl of cereal, read the paper and take Russell to the dog park."

"Perfect," HE said. "I'm looking forward to just laying around the pool today.

I went about my morning. SIR returned by 10:30. After I sucked HIM off HE got ready to take a swim. The temperature was expected to climb to 105. I hoped HE didn't expect me to sit out in the sun with HIM. I'm sure most subs would enjoy sitting around the pool with their SIR but I have pale white skin that cannot tolerate the sun. It was these kinds of compromise situations that always hindered my recent relationships. At this morning hour it was already 92 degrees. SIR stepped into the pool and swam. "Are you coming in?" HE said after a lap.

"I'll come in. But I can't get my head wet." I didn't put a t-shirt on like I normally would when I swam in the day. I didn't want HIM to think I was too eccentric just yet.

SIR continued to swim laps as I stepped into the water. HE swam up to me. "How come you can't get your head wet?"

"My ears. I can't get water in my ears."

"What about ear plugs?"

"It's not worth the risk."

"People wear them all the time."

I hated having to justify my decisions. Or explain them. Years of ear infections had made me cautious. "I just don't trust it. It takes weeks for an infection to end." I swam along the wall to keep the splashing from other people away. Already the sun beat down and I knew it was enough for me. SIR got out a few minutes after I did. We sat in the shade and read for a while.

"I'm going in again. This is heaven," HE said. "I haven't relaxed like this in a long time."

I was glad HE felt that way. Perhaps HE'd come back out. HE didn't seem to be in any rush to leave.

"Let's go up and have a little nap. Then SIR will want lunch."

Toasted tuna fish sandwiches were served at a shaded table by the pool. The afternoon went by quickly. We both read. I took Russell back to the dog park before I grilled chicken breasts for dinner with baked potatoes on The Camp's propane grill.

"That was delicious," HE said. Then added, "I need to get ready to leave."

"Do YOU think YOU'll be back out anytime soon?"

"I don't know. I'm busy with work. We'll have to see."

"We'll have to see?" HIS words stung sharper than any instrument from the night before. "That doesn't sound very positive. I thought we hit it off pretty well."

"We did. I had a great time. I never expected it to be so good."

There was silence.

"Am I going to see YOU again?"

"I don't know. Probably. I can't say for sure right now."

"Wow. I just feel that YOU might walk out that door and drive home and I'll never hear from YOU or see YOU again."

"Isn't that the case with anyone when you first meet?"

"Yes. But I don't do what I did last night with just anybody."

"Oh you must meet guys all the time for sex."

"I don't do what I did last night though."

"Well, you let me do it. This could be the start."

I didn't know what to say. I couldn't understand what was coming over me. Suddenly, I felt sad. This was why I didn't let these things happen again. My partner had spoiled me. Good sex led to relationships. I couldn't help it. I never was able to separate the two. I couldn't believe what HE was saying. Why would HE be so noncommittal? We had spent all day together. It was more than sex. It seemed to me we liked being together.

"I want you to go upstairs and pack my things."

I didn't know what to do. Continue or resist. Bastard, I thought. I pushed the chair out, stood and walked up to the room. I angrily, but neatly, packed up HIS things. A few minutes later HE opened the door. HIS bags were ready.

"Now carry them down to the car. I need to get back to LA. I was already here longer than I thought I would be."

That was nice to hear but it didn't guaranty a second encounter. I followed HIM down to HIS car. HE opened the trunk and I placed HIS two bags in. We hugged. SIR smacked my butt. Then it happened. Tears. I couldn't bear to see HIM go.

"There's no reason for tears. You've done this a thousand times."

"I know. I know. I can't help it. You're driving away. I might not ever see you again. This is what I feel."

"Well, it's crazy. We don't know each other. Let's just see what happens. What we had was good. Hold on to that." SIR got in HIS car and drove out of the parking lot.

I went back up to the room, back to the scene. There was the suitcase and the bag of chains and the furniture still rearranged. I sat down on the bed and reminisced about the night before and the whole weekend. What could these tears really mean? Was it SIR or was it finally allowing myself to experience the kind of sex I've wanted for a long time? I lay back on the mattress and looked up at the bolts in the ceiling and could see my arms extended up and out. I could feel SIR circling my body wondering where HE'd strike next. I closed my eyes and dozed off remembering HIS smell and taste and voice.

CHAPTER SIX

Birthday Whacks

I let a couple of days go by and tried not to be obsessed with checking the Leather site to see if HE had left a message. Admittedly, I did check it a few times each day and it wasn't to look for sex. It was too soon for that. I was still basking in what we had done. Though now I also felt embarrassed about the departure. I had never thrown myself on anybody before. But something in my gut and my heart said this was the one. It didn't make sense but I was determined to pursue this one.

Finally, after five days I couldn't refrain from writing, "SIR, just wanted to check in to see how YOU were. Sorry I was so needy when YOU left. I'm doing better now. Enjoyed spending time with YOU. Hope I get another chance to serve YOU. SIR's subhole."

The next day SIR responded. "SIR is happy to hear the subhole has calmed down. SIR enjoyed HIMSELF also."

I was thrilled SIR had responded. My worse fear had not come true though it would have been nice if HIS message had been longer. But maybe that was expecting too much. This was a sufficient start and soothed my anxiety. Certainly, my initial reaction was to respond immediately but I didn't want to scare HIM off any further, or worse, turn HIM off.

A few days later I sent SIR another message. "Thinking about YOU, SIR. Hope YOU are well. Any plans for Memorial Day?" SIR's subhole.

It took a couple of days. "SIR is fine. Hope the subhole is fine, too. SIR is busy over Memorial Day."

HE wasn't a man of many words that was evident. I tried not to read too much into SIR being busy. But it grated on my insecurities that a return visit was not brought up. People plan their holidays in advance, I told myself. Of course HE's busy. I decided that I would hang out at The Camp or one of the other resorts.

The weeks passed and I threw myself into my workouts, got Russell to the dog park just after sunrise and got him his first "desert shaved" haircut. It's not a shave but more than a trim and made him look like a puppy again, and planned my summer escape trip. August in the desert is unbearable. Even with a humidity of only thirty percent, when it's 109, the combination is brutal. When moving to the desert my plan was to always leave for most of August, either to Cape Cod or up to San Francisco.

No matter what I did, I couldn't get SIRManTop out of my head. Day after day I resisted contacting HIM until I could no longer restrain myself. "Hello SIR. Hope YOU are well. subhole's birthday is coming up in a week. Would it please SIR to come out and spend the weekend?" I knew this was risky but I went for broke.

A day later this message came. "It would please SIR to come out for that weekend. Can subhole get the same room?"

Ecstatically I wrote back, "Yes SIR." My turn to be brief.

"Does subhole have a harness?" HE replied later that night.

The correspondence went back and forth. "Not anymore, SIR."

"SIR plans to stay for two nights. Subhole should have food for dinner on Saturday and Sunday night. Get plenty of Gatorade."

"YES SIR. Thank YOU, SIR."

"What are the three things subhole has been trained to say?"

"Thank You SIR. Yes SIR. Subhole's only purpose is to please the SIR."

"That's right subhole. Don't forget that. And take care of your dog."

As before, I got the room ready in the early afternoon. This time there was no drama with Russell. He was thoroughly walked and settled. I waited for SIR as ordered: On my knees. Naked. By the chair. With my head facing down. I heard the door open and SIR's footsteps across the room. My pulse quickened when HE sat down in HIS chair.

"What's your only purpose?"

"Subhole's only purpose is to serve the SIR."

"That's right. I want you to be a grateful subhole this weekend. I held back last time. There'll be no mercy for mistakes this time."

"Yes SIR."

"There are lots of boys out there looking for a SIR."

"Yes SIR."

"Take SIR's boots off."

"YES SIR. Thank YOU SIR." I unlaced HIS right boot and pulled it off.

"Easy." SIR smacked me with HIS riding crop. "Don't yank it. Slide it off gently, subhole."

"Yes SIR. Thank YOU SIR." I should have known from our previous time.

I loosened the lacings and SIR's boot slipped off. I carefully placed it to the side of the chair.

"That's better."

"Yes SIR."

The second boot slipped off easily and I stood it upright next to the other boot.

"Now the socks. Get down there and smell SIR's socks."

"Yes SIR. Thank YOU SIR."

HIS socks smelled not much different from a jock strap. "Thank YOU, SIR."

"Now take them off. Gently."

"Yes SIR." Slowly I grabbed hold of the top of the sock and slid it down by SIR's ankles. With the other hand I took hold of the toe and together pulled it off HIS foot. "Thank YOU SIR."

Having done it once, the second sock came off easily. "Thank YOU SIR."

"Now get down there and massage my feet."

"Yes SIR."

"You better do a good job."

"Yes SIR." It wasn't that intimidating a task. I was good at massage. Not an expert but could comfortably hold my own. I knew better than to just jump in and squeeze. With massage, everyone has a favorite style. Figuring that out is the first step. With both hands I took hold of SIR's right foot and kneaded my thumbs into the instep of HIS foot. SIR remained quiet and I looked up to see HIM leaning back, watching me.

"Keep going subhole. What do you say?"

"Thank YOU SIR."

"I want you to be a grateful subhole."

Slowly, using all my fingers I made my way up to the ankle. Then, using just my thumbs I gratefully massaged SIR's heel. It felt rough and I wished I had some lotion. I made a mental note to use some later. With my fingers I pushed into the arch of SIR's foot. On me this area is very sensitive. I have to be completely relaxed to enjoy anyone touching me here.

SIR didn't make any motion so I pushed harder. I shifted hand positions and used my thumbs, digging deeper into the soft tissue. I moved to the balls of SIR's feet, massaging sideways across the foot. Finally I worked on SIR's toes, together, and then individually, one at a time.

"Thank YOU SIR."

"Good work, subhole. Now the other one."

Pleased, I followed the same pattern, since SIR seemed to enjoy this. I paid attention to the pressure, not going too fast, and not getting sloppy with my work. "Thank YOU, SIR."

"Good work, subhole. Now take off SIR's pants."

"Yes SIR. Thank YOU SIR." I pulled HIS sweatpants from the waist down to just above the knees. "Thank YOU SIR." Then I slid the legs out from HIS feet. This enabled me to slide one leg off from HIM. Then I got the second leg free. "Thank YOU, SIR." I folded SIR's pants and placed them next to HIS boots.

"Now get over here and lick SIR's crotch."

Back in familiar territory I had to be careful not to get too excited. I started on the right side. It was sweaty and salty. When I licked under HIS balls it was pungent. I worked my way to the other side and both our cocks were erect. I took a chance and ran my tongue along SIR's shaft, starting at the top and down to the base. I glided back to the beginning and did one more slower lap. I licked the piss hole of HIS cock several times then opened my mouth and maneuvered the head inside. Using my tongue and lips I worked the bulbous tip of SIR's mandick. Opening my mouth wide, I took in the first half of HIS cock. I drew out then slid it further down my throat until it hit the back. I felt my desire escalating. I opened wider and took all of SIR's dick, careful not to let HIM feel any of my teeth. I stretched as wide as possible and sucked HIS cock in and out. As my throat loosened I propelled more of SIR's meat into my throat hole.

"What do you say, subhole?"

I had to control myself. "Thank YOU SIR," I said, breathing heavily.

"Are you a grateful subhole?"

"Yes SIR. Thank YOU, SIR."

SIR grabbed my head, stuck HIS dick deep down in my throat and held HIS hand there. I relaxed and tried to let air in.

HIS cock grew long and thick as HE choked me with it. I didn't panic, secure with my cock sucking skills. I had done this hundreds and hundreds of times. I was actually quite pleased that

SIR took pleasure in this proclivity. It's not easy to find guys sadistic enough to satisfy the pleasure I receive from this kind of cocksucking. I saw it as a challenge, in two ways, first to see how long I could go before a gag reflex kicked in. Second, I enjoyed seeing how long a guy would go before he released my head and pulled away. It's a turn on to see a Top use my mouth and throat for their pleasure. I get aroused hearing the moans and quickening of the breath that leads to a cock exploding this way.

SIR maintains HIS head lock. In my mind I can see the seconds click by on a clock. HE holds for a good twenty seconds while I focus on not breathing and not panicking. Then SIR released HIS hold.

Gasping for air, I mumbled, "Thank YOU, SIR."

Suddenly HE said, "SIR is ready for a jacuzzi."

It startled me to hear this. Last time we had sex first. Why weren't we having sex first?

HE must have noticed my expression because HE said, "SIR has had a long stressful week. SIR needs a jacuzzi."

"Yes SIR." I lowered my head.

"What is subhole's only purpose?"

"Subhole's only purpose is to serve the SIR."

"That's right. SIR will decide what SIR wants. Not subhole."

"Yes SIR."

"Now get the towels. Or we won't have sex after either." SIR opened the door. "And bring two cans of beer."

I grabbed the towels off the counter where I had carefully placed them as instructed and draped them over my shoulder. From the cooler I removed the two cans of beer and trailed HIM a few feet behind.

SIR stepped into the jacuzzi and pointed to HIS neck. I knew what that meant. Gratefully, I sat by the perimeter of the spa and slowly dug my fingers into the thick tight muscle. SIR's head extended forward as I burrowed deeper, then gently kneaded this area. The more I worked the edges of HIS neck and massaged across the broader mass the more SIR's head lowered. "Thank YOU SIR."

"You're welcome subhole."

HE raised HIS head with a smile. "SIR will have a beer now."

"Yes, SIR." I flipped opened the tab to hand it to HIM but noticed that HE had tilted HIS head back the other way and opened HIS mouth wide.

I brought the can to HIS lips and poured a small amount into HIS mouth. "Thank YOU SIR."

SIR leaned HIS head back down towards the water where the massaging continued. We alternated in this manner for a while. SIR finished the first can.

"Good work, subhole."

"Thank YOU, SIR."

"SIR is feeling better. Open up that other can."

I obeyed HIS wishes. Soon SIR drank the second can, too, which surprised me. He didn't have any alcohol the first time. Then SIR stood. "This way, subhole."

I followed HIM to the small grass area at the back of the resort.

"On your knees, subhole."

With the resort mostly empty I knew we were alone and felt no sense of being self-conscious. I obeyed and knelt directly in front of HIM. HE held HIS cock out away from HIS body. A stream of warm piss shot out and cascaded across my smooth chest and stomach where it dripped down along my crotch. No one had ever pissed on me before. Guys had drunk my piss at the Bolt, an ancient bar on Folsom, the first bar I ever went into in San Francisco. I was underage, 19, and they never had a doorman checking ID's. Then, at party for the California Motorcycle Club Carnival, known as the CMC, an infamous bikers' bash, initially held at the former Seaman's Hall south of South of Market, I pissed on a guy on the dance floor/sex room down in the lower level. An inch of water, from spilled beer and piss, lay on the floor as the horde of drunken sweaty men danced and sexed.

Tonight was different. It was my turn to be showered and my cock roared to life. SIR sprayed HIS piss over my shoulders where it washed down my back and arms. Then it hit my face and I closed my eyes and the wet warm liquid hit my nose and forehead and cheeks. "Lean forward," HE said.

When I did HIS piss hit my head saturating my hair. HE rubbed my scalp and lathered it with HIS piss shampoo. This was HOT. Piss dripped down my head, over my ears and on all sides of my body.

"Open your mouth, subhole."

SIR's piss tasted warm and salty and filled my oral hole. I wasn't sure whether I should let it dribble out or swallow it. In hopes of pleasing HIM, I swallowed some. I couldn't believe I had finally done it. At first it took my breath away and I gasped, "Thank You SIR." Then I gulped it all without losing a drop.

Suddenly, the flow ceased. "What do you say, subhole?"

"Thank YOU, SIR."

SIR's tool was thick and hard, and aimed for my mouth. I opened it and SIR shoved it down my eager wide throat. HE drew out and plowed forward, HIS cock like a piston, drilling a hole. HIS thick legs driving with a precision-like thrust.

When I could, I muttered, "Ohh. Thank YOU SIR."

The face fuck machine continued grinding for a while. Sweat dripped from SIR's brow and drizzled down HIS jaw.

"Go up and get SIR a condom and lube," HE ordered, stepping back.

I found myself falling further under HIS spell. I leaped up and raced up the stairs, tumbling on two of them. I couldn't help but giggle a bit at my awkwardness. HE shouted something but it was indistinguishable to me. It took a few tries to fit the key into the door. Once inside, I grabbed a condom, hurried back down the stairs and presented SIR with an opened condom packet. HE rolled his eyes and shook HIS head, then wrapped HIS cock and continued with HIS piston production on my other hungry hole. HE fucked fast and furious.

I gripped the bench and held my ass out for HIM. It didn't take long for HIM to explode HIS load in my hole.

"Now stand up and turn around," HE said.

I followed my order.

SIR pinched my nipples and twisted them hard. "Stroke your dick," HE demanded.

My cock hardened. "Ohh. Thank YOU SIR." This wouldn't take long.

Still gripping them tightly, HE stepped aside as I quickly shot my juice onto the grass.

Before I could even recover HE commanded, "Now go up to the room and take the paddle out of SIR's bag and place it on the chair. Then straddle yourself on the bed with your ass on the corner. SIR's going to give you half of your birthday beating now."

"Now? After I just came."

"Of course. That's when I enjoy it the most."

This was different. I froze.

"What's your only purpose?"

"To serve the SIR."

"That's right. Now get up there and be ready. The last time I came here was a disaster when I arrived. I told you you would be punished for that. You're going to pay for it now. Did you think I had forgotten or that it wouldn't be dealt with? I've been waiting to punish you for that fiasco."

I admit I was dumbfounded. Normally I would never tolerate something like this. Reluctantly, I turned and walked away, not as eager to dash up the stairs.

The pine wooden paddle was thicker and wider than a ping pong paddle. I've never liked paddles. They stung. This would not be the birthday beating I imagined.

When SIR entered, things were as HE had demanded.

"How many whacks are your punishment, subhole?"

"Don't know SIR?" I lowered my head.

"Well, how old is the subhole?"

"Forty five, SIR."

"Then how long is the punishment?"

"Forty five, SIR." My voice trailed off. This would hurt.

"SIR will administer the punishment tonight. Let's hope the second half is for a reward tomorrow."

That wasn't so bad. "Yes SIR. Thank YOU SIR."

"Count them out loud, subhole."

"Yes SIR."

"And I hope I don't have to remind you to thank SIR."

"No SIR," I said quietly.

The wooden paddle hit the center of my ass squarely.

I gripped the bed with my fingers. "Ouw. One. Thank YOU SIR."

A blow to the right cheek.

My head jerked up. "Ugh. Two. Thank you SIR."

Then the left one.

"Oohh." My cheeks stung. "Three. Thank YOU SIR." How was I going to get through this?

Two more struck, quickly.

I dug my fingers into the mattress. "Four. Five. Thank YOU SIR." My ass hurt.

"Two more coming," SIR said.

I hid my face deep in the comforter to blunt my reaction.

A sharp blow hit each cheek.

My shouts were muffled but not the burning sensation that spread up my body.

"Happy birthday, subhole."

"Thank You SIR." My face was still buried.

SIR landed the next three on the same side.

"Oww. Ten," I bitterly shouted. My birthday wish was that this was over.

"What do you say, subhole?"

I remained silent at first. "Thank you," I replied, grinding my teeth.

"Thank YOU what?"

"Thank YOU SIR."

"Next time you'll follow orders. You're lucky I didn't just walk out. Another SIR would have. I would have if I hadn't liked what I had seen. If I hadn't thought you were worth a second chance. Three more on this cheek." They landed brutally.

"Oouw." I shoved my face down into the bed to muffle my cries. HIS words were little appeasement at that moment. "Thirteen." It was agonizing. My ass burned. No one had ever beaten me like this.

"What do you say?"

"Thank you SIR," I whispered. Not a happy subhole.

HE stood between my legs. "Raise that ass."

When I did HE massaged it with HIS hand causing me to jump skittishly. Then I realized it was just the touch of HIS hand.

"Nice. Nice and red and HOT. You'll remember this. You won't make this mistake again. Will you?"

"No SIR."

As HE continued to touch my ass with HIS hand I caught my breath.

"Four more right from here."

I burrowed into the bed to brace myself for these.

Whack to one cheek. A second to the other. Then repeated.

"The count?" SIR demanded.

"Seventeen." I was close to tears now.

"What do you say?"

"Thank YOU SIR," I sniffled.

"You thought you got away with it. Didn't you? Four more."

I closed my eyes. I could take four more. The end was close.

The first one struck wickedly searing my scorched cheek.

"How many?"

"Eighteen."

A second one enflamed my ass.

"Nineteen."

"Stick that ass high."

I raised my lower body and another one struck and knocked me down.

"Twenty."

"UP," HE ordered.

My body slowly responded.

Bang!

I would rather walk on hot coals than feel this fire on my ass. "Twenty-one," I said hoarsely, my teeth tearing into the bedspread.

"I want to hear it. No more going easy with you."

"Thank YOU SIR."

"Last one for tonight."

It struck the center of my ass with a pinging sound and sensation. It was over. I had made it but I couldn't move.

"What do you say?"

"Thank you SIR."

"How many was that?"

"Twenty two."

"That's right. Half done. We'll finish tomorrow."

I was immobile. I didn't want to look at HIM. When I finally raised my head and turned, HE was sitting in HIS chair.

"Come over here and put your head in SIR's lap."

I crawled off the bed like a wounded animal. My ass hurt. I slinked into position and resisted putting my head on HIS lap.

"Come on. All the way. I know that wasn't easy for you to take."

Eventually, I lay my head in HIS lap.

"Now we're going to go to sleep. SIR has had a busy week and the drive out is long and stressful. Later, I might wake you up to take another jacuzzi. Put the towels by the door so you don't have to look for them when you wake up. Then get into bed."

I silently followed HIS orders but failed to fully fall into a deep sleep as a part of my mind remained on alert to HIS every movement and sound.

SIR slept through the night but woke early, around six, and we soaked and swam in the warm pre-dawn air. We watched the sun rise above the distant mountain range in the east. With my ass sore and raw, for the remainder of my birthday spanking SIR used HIS hand and it was spread out over the entire day. The first five happened that morning bent over the edge of the jacuzzi; another five, later, after breakfast, in the pool; five smacks when I served tuna salad for lunch; and five more at dinner when I cooked up chicken parmigiana. The final two, and one for good luck, came just before bedtime when SIR strung me up, beat my chest and fucked me one last time and said, "Thanks for a great day, subhole. I couldn't have asked for a better way to spend it."

On Sunday we swam, soaked, and ate. Later in the afternoon the departure went off without any emotional breakdown.

"SIR had a fantastic weekend, subhole. Good work arranging all this. I know you put a lot of time and effort into pleasing ME."

"Yes SIR. Thank YOU SIR."

"I'll see you again as soon as I can get away."

I couldn't keep my mouth completely closed. "How about July Fourth?"

"I have plans already for the Fourth.

"Oh. OK." Some dejection set in.

"I'm very busy with my own company. I can't drop what I'm doing and come out. Even though I'd enjoy it."

"I understand, SIR."

"I will be in touch with you in a few weeks." SIR pulled me into a big bear hug and smacked me hard on the butt.

I winced in HIS arms.

"Happy Birthday, subhole."

"Thank YOU SIR. I'll never forget this birthday."

I watched HIM drive away in HIS Ford pick-up with my butt stinging.

CHAPTER SEVEN

Serving SIR's Friends

After a few days of not hearing from HIM my insecurities surfaced again. I couldn't wait any longer. "Good evening SIR. Hope SIR is well," I wrote. People change plans all the time. "If SIR'S holiday plans have changed my offer is still available."

There was silence for a couple of days till finally HE wrote, "SIR's plans have not changed. SIR will contact subhole after the holiday and plan something then."

It wasn't easy to read but I accepted the situation. At least there was contact and a thought of a later date. That would have to hold me for now. I turned my attention to home, Russell and the Fourth of July.

Shortly after the holiday, I got a message from HIM. "SIR is ready to come back to the desert. What weekend can you get a room?"

Gleefully, I replied, "In two weeks, SIR."

We got the same room again and things worked out just fine. Before SIR left HE said, "You need to find something else to do to take your mind off of us when we're apart."

"Like what," I said flippantly. "I have the gym and the dog."

"What about your writing? You told me you were a columnist."

I looked away. "Maybe."

"Not maybe. That's an order. You need an outlet."

I shrugged my shoulders and remained silent. Unconvinced I said, "Yes SIR. I'll start writing again."

A few weeks later, at the beginning of August I left the desert heat to house sit for a friend in foggy San Francisco. SIR seemed surprised that I was leaving for so long. I invited HIM up and HE said HE'd come if HE could but at the last minute it turned out HE wasn't able to. We spoke on the phone on several occasions. Time in San Francisco usually flies by visiting with old friends and former stomping grounds. But this trip was different. My thoughts continued to focus on the SIR. I tried to escape my obsession on HIM by going to Blow Buddies and The Citadel but it just didn't work. I compared every guy with my SIR and no one could replace HIM. I couldn't wait for August to end to return home to the desert.

I invited HIM out for Labor Day but once again HE already had other arrangements. All these holiday plans, I wondered. It seemed HE had someone special in HIS life. Memorial Day. July Fourth. Labor Day. Only a partner or serious boyfriend would take up all these days without altering them. There were many mysteries about this man. Many things I might not ever know. It would be wise of me not to build this up more than what it was – a sexual SIR/sub affair.

But HE did arrange to come back out a few weeks after the end of the summer holiday. Once again in room 40 we had our two nights together. It felt so natural to be serving HIM. It wasn't easy for me to keep thinking only along the sexual nature of our intimacy. The time between HIS visits were difficult and I still found myself pining for HIM. I should have known long distance relationships rarely worked out, and that is really what we had. The ninety miles between Palm Springs and LA might as well be across country. If I had lived in LA we would have had more opportunities to see each other and get to know each other.

Despite this, I chose to hold on for a while longer, trying to fill the time in between with the gym, the dog, my garden, and some property management that I had taken on for some extra money. And, I followed SIR's command and started writing again. My first column went into the local paper. HE was right. It did help me with our time apart. It felt good to be writing again. I had given it up when I became frustrated up north when month in and month out my closest relationship was with my computer monitor. But now, in a new location, with SIR around, it was the right time to start again.

It was in October that I first saw an advertisement about the Palm Springs Leather Pride, happening over the second weekend in November. A good move, I thought. One week after gay pride so only the serious would come.

That night I sent this email. "SIR, Leather Pride is the second weekend in November. Would it please SIR to come out for the weekend?"

An hour later, after thinking about it some more I sent this email. "SIR, the resort will probably be full that weekend. We'd either have to pay for the room. Or stay at my house."

With trepidation I awaited HIS response. I wasn't too optimistic. This would be a huge step. One HE didn't seem interested to take. Two nights later SIR responded. "It would definitely please SIR to come out for Leather Pride. SIR prefers to stay at the resort. Will there be anyone else around at your house?"

"No SIR. No one else will be at my house. I bought out my roommate. I live alone."

Two nights later HE wrote, "It will please SIR to spend the weekend at subhole's house. What is the schedule?"

HIS response put a smile on my face. "Registration is on Thursday night. There's a meet and greet mixer early Friday night.

Followed by the Tool Shed Parking Lot Party. It usually gets a big crowd and can be an easy way to meet other guys. Saturday's the contest. Then on Sunday there's a BBQ Pool party at Helios."

"Some of these look interesting to SIR. Some of them don't. SIR will decide what we will do as it gets closer. What does the subhole have to wear? It's time for subhole to get that new harness. If SIR is going to take HIS sub out in public, subhole had better look his best. How are your workouts going?"

We emailed back and forth over the next few nights. "Great SIR. I've gained another three pounds."

"Good work subhole."

"What are you at now?"

"185 SIR."

"Good work. Now get that harness."

Then I got this message. "It would please SIR if subhole hired someone to clean the house. SIR does not like messy dirty houses. It had better be neat and clean for SIR. SIR might invite some friends over to use HIS sub. You know that SIR enjoys this."

HIS response didn't surprise me. HE enjoyed groups. This wouldn't be the first time HE invited someone to join us. The last two times at the resort SIR brought others into the room to fuck me. I couldn't tell who they were because I was strung up and blindfolded. In fact, because I take my hearing aids out when I play, I didn't even know anyone was there in the room until I felt someone's warm breath behind me, as well as someone touching me from the front. Now SIR is an amazing Master, but even HE isn't able to be in two places at once. My initial reaction was to recoil in offense and rebellion.

"Stand still subhole," SIR said in a stern voice. "What is subhole's only purpose?"

I remained silent and withdrawn, unable to see SIR's face. How could HE be doing this?

"What is subhole's only purpose?" HE asked again, slowly and emphatically.

There was no point resisting. In a whisper, I responded, "subhole's only purpose is to serve the SIR."

"Say it louder," HE demanded. HIS voice rose. The words came out quicker, as though HIS patience was being frayed.

Keeping my head low, I replied, "Subhole's only purpose is to serve the SIR."

"That's right. Now stand up tall and say it again. Like you mean it."

I took a long deep breath and exhaled slowly. My body rose to full height. "Subhole's only purpose is to serve the SIR."

"Now stick that muscle ass of yours out. SIR wants to see it get used."

I obeyed and stuck my ass out a bit.

"What do you say subhole?"

"Thank YOU SIR."

"That's right. subhole should be grateful SIR is letting another Master use HIS sub. Now stick that sub hole out for SIR's friend. Just like you would if it was SIR behind you. You're doing this to please me. Isn't that what your only purpose is?"

"Yes SIR. Thank YOU SIR." I extended my ass out further.

A big unknown cock barged its way into my hole. It felt big and tight. I usually like big cocks but this one felt invasive.

"Open that hole up, subhole. SIR knows you like big cocks to fuck you. Show SIR how good you are at getting fucked. SIR enjoys watching another HOT Master using HIS sub."

"Yes SIR. Thank YOU SIR." I stuck my ass out and focused on relaxing.

The big invasive cock slammed into my ass. This stranger fucked me hard and deep.

"What do you say, subhole?"

At first I gritted my teeth. "Thank You SIR."

"Like you mean it. This is part of your training, subhole. What's your only purpose?"

"To serve the SIR."

"Then do it. Show ME how grateful you are? I want to hear it."

"Thank YOU SIR," I said loudly.

The stranger's cock seemed to grow with our exchange. His moans filled the room. I heard him grunting then he cried out "I'm gonna shoot," as he fucked my ass faster and wildly.

"Shit. That was fuckin' hot," he said as his big cock slipped out of my hole.

I was glad it was over but now my butt felt empty.

I heard the stranger thank the SIR and the door closed.

Then SIR stood in front of me. "Good work subhole. SIR is pleased. That was HOT."

"Thank You SIR," I said quietly.

"What's your only purpose?"

"To please the SIR."

"That's right. And that pleased the SIR. That's all that matters." I could hear SIR opening up a wrapper. HE stepped behind me and stuck HIS cock in me.

"Thank YOU SIR," I said quietly.

"What's subhole's only purpose?"

"To serve the SIR."

"That's right. Subhole will do whatever the SIR tells him to do."

HIS cock grew inside me.

"Yes SIR. Thank YOU SIR."

"Whatever the fuck SIR tells him to do. Uggh. Fuck. Yeah. Whatever the fuck SIR says. Ohh. Yeah. Stick that ass." SIR stood still, continuing to breath heavy.

"Thank YOU SIR."

HIS cock slipped out and it was jacuzzi time.

Then this last time HE came out for a weekend we wandered around the resort and in the area off to the side SIR said, "On your knees, subhole."

I obeyed, waiting in position with my arms behind my back.

SIR found several guys who took turns fucking my face. Then HE ordered me to stand up and while I continued to suck off these strangers SIR fucked my ass. Having both holes filled at the same time was pretty fucking exciting.

So when SIR said HE might invite guys over to the house it wasn't such a surprise. But a stranger coming to my house was different than fucking with someone at the resort. This would be a stretch for me.

A friend suggested that I buy my new harness in LA. He even offered to drive in with me one afternoon and we checked out 665. Eddie, a hot ripped guy covered with tattoos from the neck down, which I actually recognized from some leather porn videos that I had beaten off to, introduced himself.

I told him my SIR ordered me to get a harness for Leather Pride. He laughed and said, "Take off your shirt."

I slipped my arms out. He grabbed it and threw it onto the counter and it slid off onto the floor. Then he said, "Nice chest."

I nodded my head self-consciously. "Thanks. I've been working out hard."

"It shows." He turned to my friend and told him to wait at the counter while he led me to the back of the shop.

He pulled several harnesses off the racks. One required that I pull down my pants. He slipped the cock ring around my balls and pulled the strap between my legs. That's when I got a hard-on.

Standing behind me he grabbed my dick and stroked it. "I think this harness will please your SIR."

I admired myself in the mirror. I knew he was right. Then his head disappeared behind my shoulders. I felt his tongue licking the lower part of my back. His hands grabbed my cheeks and spread them wide. I thrust out my ass and his tongue slipped into my hole. I shot out of control all over the mirror.

Back at the front of the store, I said to my friend, "I got the right one."

Eddie handed me back my shirt from behind the counter. "Definitely. It looks hot," he said.

"Do I get a discount?" I asked with a laugh.

"You sure do."

I watched him slide the harness into a bag and use his finger to wipe off the left over cum.

As we walked out of the shop I thanked my friend for bringing me to 665, and said, "I think I'm ready for Leather Pride now."

CHAPTER EIGHT

Leather Pride Weekend

A week before Leather Pride SIR wrote that HE would be in Palm Springs Friday night at nine and that I was to be dressed in my chaps, jock strap, and new harness for SIR's inspection before going to the parking lot party.

With a clean house I waited for HIM on my knees.

"Let's see that new harness on you subhole," SIR said, when he came through the front door.

"That looks HOT, subhole. Good choice."

"Thank YOU SIR."

November nights can be chilly for the locals, used to the desert heat. "SIR, may I have permission to make a request?"

"Yes subhole. You have permission to make a request."

"May I wear my jeans? It's cold."

"Yes, subhole. You have permission to wear jeans. But not a shirt. And put on this yellow armband that I brought for you."

"Yes SIR." It's been a long while since I had displayed my sexual preferences in public. Showing my fetishes with SIR, in my small home town, made me slightly self-conscious but not too uncomfortable as long as HE was next to me.

SIR changed into HIS black jeans and a leather shirt.

"You look very HOT and handsome SIR."

"Thank YOU, subhole. Now let's go."

We arrived at the Tool Shed and the crowd was thick. Most people stood under one of several portable heaters the organizers wisely provided. After we waited in line for our drinks we joined the warm leather revelers.

While I'm more of the nod and smile guy, SIR immediately started a conversation with two guys standing next to us. As the conversation continued longer than expected, I sized up the two strangers. One stood a foot above the crowd. He was older with short buzzed grey hair and his thick beard was also speckled with grey hairs. He wore a black T-shirt and a leather vest and leather pants. He wasn't muscular but definitely not out of shape either. If I were single I'd definitely give him a second look. His buddy was shorter, younger than all of us, with buzzed blond hair with a goatee. He dressed in the same outfit as me with a harness, no shirt, and chaps. The only difference was he wasn't wearing anything under his chaps so his dick and ass were exposed. His butt was probably freezing and just looking at him made me shiver. I was grateful I didn't have to dress like that. From where I stood his ass was out of view so I didn't know what it looked like. But if it was anything like the rest of him it was firm and round because he definitely was cute. Not as muscular as I was but younger and his chest was smooth as well as his washboard stomach. Over his cock was a plastic chastity case. SIR and the bearded guy talked about him as though he were a piece of meat.

"This is my sub," SIR finally said, nodding in my direction.

A thrill of goose bumps washed over my body that wasn't from the chilly air. Then SIR put HIS arm around me and drew me in close. With HIM, my self-consciousness faded and I was proud to be seen standing next to HIM. It was also warmer with HIS arm around me.

"He's a sexy boy," the bearded one said.

"He certainly is. And he's well trained."

"I'd like to see how well trained he is." He added, "Perhaps we could share our slaves for a while."

"That is definitely a possibility. I'd enjoy using your slave and am definitely into watching my sub serve you." SIR looked towards me. "What do you think subhole? Would you enjoy serving Master Tom?"

I knew the appropriate answer but the idea of watching SIR having sex with someone else didn't seem like fun. I'm not a sharing kind of bottom. But I know how SIR wanted me to answer. "Yes SIR. I would enjoy that. Whatever pleases YOU, SIR?"

"Oh, you do have him well trained," the bearded one said. To his slave buddy he said, "Did you hear that? Whatever pleases you, SIR? Without any prompting. That's how I want you to respond."

His slave just smiled.

I knew how he felt but I was pleased to show off to the younger guy. Maybe age does give you some wisdom.

"SIR's a little tired tonight. How about tomorrow night?"

"That sounds right. What other events are you going to? You going to the contest tomorrow night?" the Beard asked.

"We'll go late. I find contests to be dull."

"I agree but the boy here has never been to one before so I'm taking him. Why don't we meet tomorrow night and see if it works out. I would definitely enjoy using and abusing your slave."

"That sounds like a good plan," SIR said.

After good-byes we wandered around the parking lot one more time checking out the booths and getting a second beer, before finding another warm spot to pause. I was relieved nothing had come of the encounter. Was I ready for some young stud to be having sex with my SIR? No, I was not.

Under the warmth of the portable heater we smiled and nodded at other guys standing near us. I recognized a few faces from the gym and the dog park. I nodded at a couple of acquaintances from the Palm Springs Leather Order of the Desert, the group putting on the Leather Pride Weekend.

"I think you ought to join the Leather Club," SIR said.

I remained silent. Clubs hadn't turned out so well.

"I think it's the perfect club for you."

"I don't know. Maybe."

"Not maybe. That's an order. I want you to join so we'll know about the events they put on. Wait here. I'm going to go get a brochure from their table."

SIR walked away. HE spent a few minutes talking to the guys manning their booth. When HE returned HE handed me the brochure, "They have a meeting the first Wednesday of every month. I want you to go to the next one and join. They'll be happy to have a guy like you."

Folding the flyer in half and stuffing in into my back pocket, I remained quiet. From the warmth of the heater we watched the crowd pass by.

"SIR is ready to leave," HE eventually said.

"Yes SIR." I was relieved to have SIR all to myself.

On the drive home I asked, "Would SIR like to go for a jacuzzi?"

"At the resort? Can we get in if we're not staying there?"

"Yes SIR. Anytime we want. I go whenever my body's sore from my workouts. I just check in at the front to let 'em know I'm there."

"Fantastic. SIR would love a jacuzzi. Good idea subhole."

"Thank YOU, SIR."

When I opened my eyes and SIR was in the bed, in my room, and in my house, I was thrilled, and, it was a bit of a reality shock. Now I couldn't just go down stairs to the breakfast room of the resort and get HIM coffee and a muffin. Now there's breakfast to think about. We'd already discussed my lack of coffee making since I only drink tea.

"SIR will go to Starbuck's for coffee. When I come back I expect breakfast to be ready. SIR likes HIS two eggs over easy."

"Yes SIR. Thank YOU SIR."

While SIR was gone I got the bacon into the skillet and the eggs ready to fry. I fed Russell so he was taken care of. I'm sure he was equally surprised someone spent the night and was staying in the morning. It's a cool clear calm day so I placed a nice tablecloth over the patio table and set out two good placemats and cloth napkins.

"I smell bacon," SIR shouted when HE returned. HIS voice filled the house. It was strange to hear another voice. Strange but exciting.

"Just about ready."

HE had the New York Times and immediately went outside and sat at the table. He seemed to have expected the arrangement.

I'm a good cook when it comes to just myself. But I feel pressure when it's more than one. I start to get anxious, thinking the bacon will be burnt or the eggs too hard.

"How do you like your bacon, SIR?"

"Medium well, boy."

I'm not sure whether the bacon is medium or medium well so I carried a piece out to HIM. "Is this good?"

"Perfect! Good work."

Relief settled over me and after the eggs turned out perfect, too, we were ready to eat.

While we ate, SIR said, "What a beautiful garden, subhole. Did you do this?"

"Yes SIR. I did. It was barren when I bought the place. I'll show you pictures of how ugly it was. The old lady who had it wanted shade and low maintenance. I kept the shade but I had to bring in plants."

"It's so relaxing here. I can't believe it. I like the way you have tall cactus in between all the smaller bushes."

"It's really pretty in the spring when things are blooming."

"I can't wait to see it."

HIS comment brought a wide smile to my face.

"And all the bird sounds," HE added.

"Yeah, I've created a little oasis here. There's seven or eight different species. Some are migratory. Just here for the winter. Some are year round."

"Do you know what they are?"

"I have an idea. I keep a couple of bird books around. That one right there. With the orange chest. That's a grosbeak. He comes twice a year. Now and in the spring."

"That's amazing. How do you know so much?"

"I had an acre of land in the redwoods up north with a great garden. I had lots of birds there too."

"It's sounds beautiful. Why did you leave?"

"I needed to be around more people. I needed to let go of that house that my partner and I bought. I wasn't going to find a relationship up there in that house."

"Well, you got a great set-up here, subhole."

"Tha..."

"When I'm done changing a few things around it's even going to be better."

His words hit me like one of the birds in Alfred Hitchcock's movie. This is what I hated about relationships. This is why they hadn't worked out. I treaded lightly. "What changes are you suggesting, SIR?"

"Nothing major. How come you haven't painted this patio? It'll look much better with some color."

I sat in silence for a moment remembering how when you close one door, the changes come in surprising places. I invited this; invited him. I inhaled and tried not to get upset. He must have noticed my reaction.

"You can throw down two coats of paint in no time at all. It's so beautiful out here why wouldn't you take this final step."

"I hadn't thought of it, SIR. I'm not a decorating kind of guy."

"Don't give SIR that line. You painted the inside great. A little paint will go a long way. You'll be glad you did. Get some paint samples and the next time I'm here I'll pick out a color."

I stayed quiet.

"That's an order," SIR said and the issue was closed. "SIR will now get back in bed and when subhole is finished cleaning up he'll come join me and suck my dick. Understand?"

"Yes SIR."

After cleaning up the breakfast dishes I joined SIR in the bedroom.

"In between my legs, subhole. That's where you belong."

Having someone in my house ordering me took some getting used to. But I obeyed. It actually made me giggle a little to climb in between HIS thick legs. Like a joey climbing into the pouch. I laid my head next to HIS cock. Suddenly, I realized I could get very used to this.

"Now do a good job and suck SIR's dick."

I took it in my open mouth and SIR's dick grew.

I stopped. "SIR, do I have permission to shoot?"

"No. We got a long day ahead. There'll be plenty of time for the boy to shoot. I want you primed."

It didn't take long for SIR to shoot a big load into my mouth. That's when we drifted off for a nap; with me still between HIS legs.

After a short time Russell whined outside the door. He did that when he wasn't getting enough attention so I slipped out from under the covers.

"Where are you going?"

"I'm gonna check up on Russell. I heard him making noises. I should take him to the dog park."

"That's a good idea. I have some calls to make. When you come back I want to go somewhere for a swim."

"Okay. We can go to the resort if that pleases YOU, SIR?"

"That would please ME. Hurry back."

It was two o'clock by the time we got ready to go over to Camp Palm Springs. "I want you to swim today," SIR said.

"I can't." I turned and looked away.

"What do you do when you shower?"

"I put cotton and Vaseline in my ears."

"Do you get an infection?"

"No."

"Well then, that's what I want you to do today. Even if it's just for a few laps."

I didn't know what to say. It's been so long since I swam, really swam. "Fine. I'll try it, SIR." Perhaps HE's right and it will be like showering. Arguing with HIM doesn't seem useful. I might as well try it. I did want someone who wouldn't roll over so easily in a discussion.

When we arrived at Camp Palm Springs it was crowded with other hot leather men, many of whom we saw at the Tool Shed the night before. I'm glad we didn't get a room. Even the pool is packed with men.

SIR dropped HIS clothes and dove in. By the time I blocked my ears and waded into the water SIR was on an air mattress with a young bearded muscle guy at the edge of the float eyeing SIR's growing dick. I was really glad that I was in the water. Without thinking about my ears I dove towards SIR's raft and emerged on the other side.

SIR looked at me and said, "Subhole, this is Bryan. He's from Texas. It's his first leather weekend."

Bryan reached across and shook my hand. "You're a lucky sub."

"Yes. I realize that," I said to him.

SIR said, "Subhole, show Bryan how to service SIR's dick."

I pulled HIS shaft to my mouth and gently licked the tip of the head and around the edges. I passed SIR's cock over to our eager friend.

Bryan took his turn, following my example. Together we joined forces and licked the shaft meeting at the base of HIS balls where out tongues touched. It didn't take long for SIR's mandick to explode all over HIS hairy stomach. I decided to let the Texan have the honor of cleaning up with his tongue.

SIR slid off the raft, into the water and swam off.

"Good luck finding your own SIR," I said to Bryan, then I immediately pursued after my SIR. I was not letting HIM out of my sight again. When I reached the deep end HE was waiting for me.

"How are your ears, subhole?"

"Fine SIR. Thank YOU for asking."

"How's it feel to be in the pool?"

"It feels great, SIR. Thank YOU."

"Subhole, if you continue to follow SIR's orders your life is going to improve."

"I would like that SIR. I have a difficult time making decisions."

"From now on before you make any decisions you run it by me. I don't want you making any decisions on your own."

I stared at this stranger who was now trying to run my life.

"You want a SIR/sub relationship or not?"

"Yes SIR."

"Well then this is how it's going to be from now on. It's been seven months. We've both had plenty of time to think about it. Your life is about to get better now that I'm in it. Both of our lives are going to be better. I've been wanting to spend more time out here. It's going to work well. You'll see."

Before SIR could swim away, I wrapped my arms around HIM. HE turned and pulled me in tight with a huge grin on HIS face.

CHAPTER NINE

Another Sub

For dinner we BBQ'd chicken on the backyard grill with baked potatoes and broccoli.

"Good food subhole. Don't eat too much, though."

"Yes SIR. I'm already feeling a bit full."

"What time is the contest?" SIR asked, after HE pushed HIS empty plate away.

"9 pm. I think?"

"We'll go around eleven. I've invited another SIR over to use you before we go."

"Who is it SIR?"

"Doesn't matter. What is your only purpose, subhole?

"To serve the SIR."

"And whoever SIR decides you serve."

"Yes SIR."

After dinner, I gave Russell some needed attention. This time we walked over to Ruth Hardy Park and threw the ball a few times. He seemed happy to have my undivided attention. As I threw the ball I wondered how SIR could have arranged this. I'd been with HIM the whole weekend.

When I returned there were blankets covering the back porch windows. SIR said, "Get your harness on and get ready. I have a muscle Daddy coming over to fuck you."

"Yes SIR." I did the sanitary things then dressed in my harness, jock strap and boots. A short time later the doorbell rang.

"He's here. Get in position, subhole."

I knelt, waiting in the back porch with my hands behind my back.

SIR walked in leading a tall muscular husky 30 year old HOT redhead with tattoos on both shoulders. "This is subhole. You can use him any way you like. He's a great cocksucker. Loves to get fucked. Punched. Nipple play. Piss. Anything you want. But don't leave any marks."

"He's a HOT boy. Look at those muscles." Red slugged my left chest.

It felt good.

"What do you say subhole?" SIR said, sporting an evil grin.

"Thank YOU SIR."

"That's right. He's a grateful subhole."

Another punch to the other side.

I liked this guy already. "Thank YOU, SIR."

Red unzipped his fly and yanked out a big uncut cock. His pubic hairs matched the hairs on his body.

I opened my mouth and he slipped his dick in. It was then that I noticed the star around his cock. He slid it in and out and it grew inside my warm hungry hole. He star banged my lips as it came and went. I was psyched.

"Do a good job, subhole." SIR stood in the doorway, observing.

"Yes SIR," the words gurgled out.

Red's dick grew to its full eight inches.

"Stand up and turn around subhole. It's time to show off that muscle ass," SIR directed.

I stood and turned around as ordered.

"Stick that ass out," SIR commanded from the sideline.

"Yes SIR." This time I would enjoy it.

Red stuck a finger in my hole and poked around. "Nice hole," he said moving up close to me. The head of his cock entered my a-hole.

He shoved it in a few inches more and it felt good. He was a big hot stud and I wanted to feel that star hitting my ass.

"You like that subhole?" SIR asked.

"Yes SIR," I said emphatically.

"I thought you might. You fuckin' whore. What do you say?"

"Thank YOU SIR."

"Are you a grateful subhole? You like that star around his cock?"

"Yes SIR," I shouted.

SIR stood in front of me. "Well show me your gratitude. Suck MY dick." HE grabbed the hair on the back of my head and dragged it down and started face fucking me brutally.

By leaning forward my ass extended out further.

"Oh yeah," Red said. "That's fuckin hot."

"Use his ass. It's all yours," SIR snarled.

I sucked SIR's hard cock while Red rammed all eight inches of his uncut fuck tool inside me. It was hard to focus on either of them but both holes got hungry for more and opened wider. I shoved my butt out towards Red, moaning, "Oh yeah. Give it to me big guy. Hit my ass with that star."

All of Red's eight thick inches slammed my hole and it took my breath away a bit.

"Thank YOU SIR," I gurgled, as SIR drew out HIS cock and rammed it back down my throat.

"Grr." Red moaned and fucked rougher.

His big husky muscular hairy body banged into my firm ass. I wanted all of Red's dick in my hole. He pumped my ass like a fucking rapid fire nail gun machine.

"I'm getting close," Red growled.

"Shoot it in his ass. In his ass. Use it as a cum dump."

"Fuck yeah. I'm close. Ugh. Fuck yeah. Yeah." Red's big body pounded up against my ass and thrust forward as he fired in his load deep. Once, twice, three times. Then his body slowed down and idled. After a pause his dick slipped out.

"Fuck. That was nice," he said, exhaling.

That's when SIR blasted HIS load down my throat.

I swallowed it all. "Thank You SIR," I said, truly a grateful subhole.

We all got what we wanted so without much talk, Red and his star dressed and left.

"Now go shower and we'll go on over to the contest," SIR said.

As we dressed to go, SIR informed me, "Bare ass, subhole. Bare ass and a jock strap."

I'd never gone out bare assed before. I wanted to protest but I knew he gave in last night and wouldn't tonight.

"Where's your new arm band? Go get it and put it on."

I found the arm band and slipped it in place.

"No slouching tonight, subhole. SIR wants you to stand tall. Your hard work has paid off. SIR is looking forward to showing off HIS subhole this evening."

I was pleased. HIS words touched me to the core. Everything I had worked for and hoped for was unfolding. With a renewed sense of confidence I followed my SIR out the door.

We arrived at The Oasis around ten. Before we entered SIR took out HIS handcuffs and restrained my hands behind my back. SIR paid the cover charge for both of us.

"That's HOT," a handsome bearded leather man, taking the money at the front booth, said, as we walked by.

SIR nodded and smiled.

The contest was still dragging on, as they often do. It's as bad as the Oscars. We listened for a brief time to some of the questions and responses. We liked a couple of the contestants and commented on which judges we knew but then moved to the back of the large hall where people were congregating in front of the silent auction tables.

We bumped into the two guys from the Tool Shed the night before and talked for a while but the energy wasn't the same so after a while we moved on. I introduced SIR to a few people that I knew from the dog park.

"We finally get to meet you," one of them said.

"We didn't think you really existed," his buddy added.

"I'm real. I don't just jump into things," SIR responded.

"Well, we think you got a good catch with this one," one of my friends said as he pointed to me.

SIR smiled. "Me too. And he's not escaping tonight." We all laughed.

Then SIR eyed a young guy off in the corner, half watching the contest and half cruising the crowd. SIR circled the guy, dressed in black chaps with his ass hanging out and a harness. A black hanky stuck out from the chaps on the right side. His head was buzzed like a marine and he had a nice defined body. Not built up like mine but definitely in shape.

SIR stepped in closer. "You look like a Marine."

"I actually am a Marine, SIR," he said in a deep voice. "I recently separated."

"Awesome." SIR became slightly animated.

Standing in the back I wasn't too pleased with the direction that this was going. SIR was about to pick up another sub. I heard them talking.

"Yes SIR," the marine said.

SIR walked over to me. "Turn around, subhole." When I obeyed, SIR released my left hand from the cuffs and pulled me over where I found myself face to face with this Marine. My pulse perked up. He was an inch shorter with a strikingly masculine tough look.

"Stick out your right hand, subhole."

I obeyed and SIR attached the open handcuff to the marine's left hand and we were led out of the building.

Once in the porch play room, SIR ordered us both to kneel down in position. HE detached the handcuffs as HE inspected us like merchandise.

"Up straight subhole."

"Yes SIR."

"Stick that ass out grunt."

"Yes SIR," he said.

I looked straight ahead but out of the corner of my eye I saw SIR stroking HIS dick and sticking it in grunt's open mouth. Grunt slurped at SIR's cock.

"What do you say grunt?"

"Thank YOU SIR."

"That's right. You're a grateful marine. Aren't you, grunt?"

"Yes SIR."

"Show SIR that gratitude and do a good job."

No longer disciplined enough to face forward I watched the grunt hungrily devour SIR's cock. Sucking it, in and out. It was arousing and disturbing.

"Get over here subhole and lick SIR's balls."

"Yes SIR." There was no point in resisting.

"And do a good job."

Sitting next to the grunt I leaned in and under them and ran my tongue against one of SIR's thick hairy balls.

HE groaned and leaned forward. SMACK. I didn't see it but I knew it was SIR's hand against the grunt's bare smooth ass.

"What do you say grunt?"

"Thank You SIR."

"That's right. Let's show him how it's done subhole. Stick that ass out."

I extended my body and SIR leaned forward. SMACK against my ass.

"Thank YOU SIR."

"That's right. That's how it's done grunt. Now let's try that again. Stick that ass out for SIR."

SMACK!

"Thank You SIR," grunt said.

"That's better."

"Stand up subhole and let the grunt suck your dick."

"Yes SIR. Thank You, SIR." I hadn't expected this.

It's been a long time since I got a blowjob and it felt good. Grunt had a good mouth, like a vacuum sucking up the crumbs. My dick grew. Taking the initiative I leaned forward and shoved two fingers into the grunt's ass hole. I'm surprised at how easily they slid in. This marine has had a few things in there before. I rammed in a third finger and my dick responded.

SIR must have noticed because HE said, "Get behind him, subhole. Show me how you used to fuck guys." To the grunt HE asked, "Should MY sub put on a condom?"

"No SIR. No need," grunt replied.

With a hard cock I positioned myself behind the grunt. Poking a few fingers in his hole up to my knuckles got my cock rock hard and it entered easily. Fucking someone felt good. SIR reached out and teased my nipples. My cock slipped out and I drove it back inside. Sometimes I do enjoy fucking a nice loose hole that has no resistance.

"That feel good, subhole?" SIR asked.

"Yes SIR." I never knew what to expect with HIM.

"Fuck his ass harder, subhole. SIR enjoys watching HIS boy fuck."

"Yes SIR. Thank YOU SIR."

"What do you say grunt?"

"Thank you SIR."

"That's right. When's the last time a muscle stud fucked your ass? You better be grateful."

"Thank You SIR."

Not having done it for over two years, it wouldn't take me long to shoot so I pulled out. "Getting close, SIR."

"Turn around grunt and clean off his dick with your mouth."

Grunt obeyed and his tongue glided across my clean cock.

"Stick your ass out again grunt. SIR's turn."

"Yes SIR. Thank You SIR."

SIR wrapped it and rammed HIS big cock into grunt's loose hole.

"Oh yeah. Nice ass grunt," HE shouted.

"Thank YOU SIR."

Having receded from the brink I shoved my cock down grunt's throat and fucked his face. But it didn't take long for me to get close again and I held his head in front of my cock. "Just lick it."

SIR continued to fuck his ass. It wasn't so bad watching HIM fuck this guy. I sort of enjoyed it.

I reached under and yanked on grunt's big nipples. When I twisted them he moaned with pleasure.

Then SIR abruptly pulled out and stepped back to catch HIS breath. "Get the restraints subhole and string him up. Time for a flogging."

"Yes SIR," I said, sadistically torn between the pleasure received from using him and also admittedly, eager to see this intruder beaten.

The toys were in the suitcase and it took a moment to find the pair. I clasped the first buckle tight around his wrist and then the second one before hooking both wrists to the bolts in the beam above.

"What do you say, grunt?" SIR demanded.

"Thank you SIR," he said.

"That's right. Show some gratitude grunt. I don't want to have to say it again."

"Yes SIR."

SIR picked up the leather flogger and glided it along grunt's back. "It's an honor to serve a SIR. Isn't that right, grunt?"

"Yes SIR."

"Then I want to hear that gratitude." SIR struck the flogger against his smooth back.

"Thank you SIR."

"That's what I want to hear." HE struck again.

"Thank you, SIR."

I kneeled at SIR's side watching the scene.

SIR switched his weapon and continued to whip grunt's back with the rubber flogger. From experience I knew this one always hurt more. There were already several red marks on his back.

"Stick that ass out boy."

"Yes SIR. Thank YOU SIR."

The flogger landed several times on his white smooth cheeks. Each time he thanked the SIR. I was surprised that my own dick hardened at the sight of each new mark on the grunt's ass.

SIR looked over and smiled. "Get over here subhole and stick that dick up his ass again."

"Yes SIR." I stood in position and fucked it hard. I pulled my cock out completely, and shoved it back, all the way in. "Ohh. Yeah," I cried out. It felt good.

At that moment I felt a sting as the flogger landed across my back.

"Thank you SIR." I slammed my cock in again.

The leather flogger struck the side of my back.

"Thank YOU SIR," I whispered. It's not easy for me to focus on both activities, an aggressive act and a submissive one. Losing its firmness, my cock slipped out and I stepped away without regret. I had my fun.

The flogger struck grunt's back.

"Thank You SIR," he said.

"Get down there subhole and suck his dick." The flogger struck him again.

"Yes SIR," I said. It didn't take long for me to get grunt's dick hard.

Now SIR has stopped. HE moved next to us and stuck HIS dick into grunt's hole. Grunt's cock grew to life in my mouth. This wouldn't take long I thought to myself.

SIR slammed into grunt's ass several times while I sucked his dick and reached up and twisted his big firm nipples.

"Ooh. Ugh," grunt cried out. "I'm close."

I sucked faster.

"I'm gonna shoot," grunt groaned.

I pulled away and grunt's juice hit my face and shoulders in machine gun fire fashion.

SIR's body heaved forward and HE fucked the Marine furiously.

"Fuck," he shouted out."Fuckin' marine. Cocksucking marine. Ugh." SIR shot HIS load into the Marine's ass. Then HE stumbled back and sat in HIS chair.

I stood and unhooked grunt. He listed slightly and I balanced him and led him to his knees in front of the SIR, where he placed his head on SIR's knee.

"Damn. That was HOT," grunt said. "Thank YOU SIR," he added.

I knelt next to him and placed my head on SIR's other knee. "Thank You, SIR."

CHAPTER TEN

Public Service

For breakfast I made crab benedict and served it out in the patio.

"This is delicious subhole."

"Thanks SIR. It's my favorite." I hoped HE'd like it.

"Where'd you get the crab?"

"Trader Joe's has canned crab meat for only eight dollars. It's pretty good."

"Good work."

"Thanks SIR." I sat back and savored the food and the moment.

"How come you don't have a bed out in the porch?"

Here we go again with questions. "I don't know SIR. I just never thought of it."

"It's the only room in the house that looks out onto this beautiful garden. What an amazing sight to wake up to every morning."

"I never thought of it SIR. There isn't any air conditioning back here. It bakes in the summer."

"Summer is over. We're going to get a mattress and put it out here for the cooler weather. I want to wake up and see this. We can take naps during the day. Lie in bed and watch the birds. Wouldn't you like that?"

"Yes SIR. It's a good idea."

"And I have some nice patio chairs I can bring out and get rid of these ugly uncomfortable ones."

When HE moves, HE moves quickly, I thought.

SIR grinned HIS mischievous smile. "What are you thinking subhole? I can tell you're thinking something. You're very transparent. You wanted this. Now you have it."

"Yes SIR. I'm pleased. It's feast or famine."

"The dam broke, now the flood starts. Now clean up these dishes. SIR wants to read the paper, and then climb back into bed for you to do your job. What time does this pool party begin?"

"Eleven. I think."

"We can go around 1. That should give us some time to swim. SIR has to head back to LA around 5 to get ready for a busy day tomorrow and a full week."

There was silence. The sounds of the birds filled the garden.

"I trust there will be no more unfortunate displays when I leave?"

"No SIR."

"Subhole has to trust that SIR plans to return as soon as HE is able."

"Yes SIR."

"No more phone calls about how much you miss ME?"

"I can't guaranty that, SIR." I said it in a lowered voice. "I'm not hiding my emotions."

"OK. That I might be able to handle. Once in a while. Up to a point."

"I trust you'll return."

"And...I also don't expect you to be monogamous while I'm away. There's no point. I want you to have fun. If you see a hot guy or if a HOT Daddy comes on to you I want you to call me and ask for permission to have sex with him. Then I want to hear about what you did."

"YOU want me to tell YOU?"

"Yes. It turns SIR on."

I sat dumbfounded.

"I'm not like those other boyfriends of yours who got all jealous and possessive. I want to hear about it."

This was not familiar territory. "YOU want me to ask permission and then tell YOU about it?"

"That's right. That's an order."

"Then I don't want sex with anyone else."

"I might not be able to come out every week. Every two weeks if I'm lucky. I don't expect, nor want you, to hold off for ME. If you see a hot SIR at the gym I want you to go after him."

"A hot SIR? At World Gym?" I said in my most sarcastic tone.

"A hot guy then. You know what I mean. Stop being rebellious. The dog park. The coffee shop. Or anywhere. Have fun. You deserve it. Just ask permission and tell me what you did. It's not that difficult."

In previous relationships, extramarital sex was always kept out of the conversation. It wasn't an issue as long as it didn't interfere. But to openly do it and talk about it was not easy for me.

"I might just not have sex then."

"You'll see. After a week or ten days you'll get horny and see someone. Any way, you have your orders. You figure it out. Now clean up these dishes."

In a sullen mood I cleaned up breakfast. All these changes, I thought. Is this really what I wanted? Or just sex? I loaded the dish washer. No, this is what I needed. Somebody who knew what he wanted, said it and then wouldn't back down. I didn't want to make these decisions alone anymore. After cleaning up I joined SIR in the bed and finished my job.

An hour later we drove over to Helios. Cars lined the road in both directions and the vacant lot next door was full, also.

"I guess this is the place to be," SIR said.

The smell of the grill permeated the air even outside the complex. I was dressed in my green cargo shorts, harness, black boots, a green ball cap to keep the sun off my face and on SIR's insistence, on my right arm, the tight yellow arm band.

SIR wore tight black leather shorts that showed his HOT thick firm butt and bulging muscular legs, a black leather vest and a black ball cap. Today I convinced him to go shirtless and show off his thick hairy chiseled chest. HE looked mighty fine to me. HE also brought along a smaller bag of toys. I wasn't sure what collection HE included.

It was wall to wall leather men of all sizes and shapes. The younger, hotter ones, guys in their thirties and forties, stood around in groups to display their hard work. We were dressed appropriately as shorts and no shirt seemed to be the standard uniform, though enough were dressed in just a harness and boots. I was relieved SIR didn't require me to dress down.

The resort buzzed with music and voices. Though it was a pool party and a warm day, not too many guys were actually in the pool. It's not easy getting in and out of all this gear.

"We'll eat first, subhole," SIR said. "You never know when they might run out of food."

SIR led us towards the back bar where the food was. The guys stepped aside and cruised SIR as we walked by. It was amusing that even the supposed tops expressed interest in HIM once they noticed HIS huge arms and hairy muscular chest.

Luckily, we found two empty chairs at a table in the shade and got a plate of chicken, corn on the cob and potato salad. I couldn't resist the brownie plate.

"This is good. I'm glad we didn't wait," SIR said. "Look at all these HOT guys. I'm glad we came. Finish eating, we're going to cruise when we're done."

I rolled my eyes but didn't say anything. Looking around I didn't recognize many faces. Not as many locals as I expected. That's a good thing if HE was out to cruise. The idea of sex in front of the locals would make me uncomfortable.

When SIR's plate was empty HE stood and was eager to hunt.

"SIR, may I have permission to make a request?"

"Yes subhole. You have permission to make a request."

"Can we please sit somewhere and digest a bit before?"

"Of course. Put these in the trash. I'll find a place on the grass to set up our towels."

I reacted quickly because in this crowd it would be easy to lose sight of HIM and I remembered how quickly things evolved yesterday at the pool. I could tell HE was in overdrive with all these muscled guys hanging around.

Again we found some room under a tree. On this warm day, in the dry desert air, without humidity, it made the temperature perfect in the shade. Helios is a great place for an event like this. It's big enough to hold a fair number of people, yet small enough for the event to be dense and intimate.

Sitting among the crowd gave me a better perspective. Not all the guys were gym guys. We were surrounded by a broad mix of older bears, hairy leather daddies, young and older thin guys and overweight, happily married couples not concerned about a little mirth and girth. Everyone seemed relaxed and carefree, except for SIR.

HE looked around, clearly restless, on the hunt. I knew what this meant and followed HIS lead. "Take the bag," HE said.

There's a separate building in the back with bathrooms and a grassy area with a St. Andrews cross set up in the corner. A few guys were getting sucked off and people watched from a distance, treating it nonchalantly, as if it were just kids in a playground.

SIR stood off to the side watching while I waited behind HIM. A few guys took notice of us as they passed. I was sure one of them would notice the yellow arm band on my right side. And suddenly, a handsome older smooth muscular daddy stood next to SIR and struck up a conversation. I heard bits and pieces.

"He's trained well. He's a fuck hole and piss hole," SIR said.

"I got a full bladder I'd like to use on him," the Pisser said.

"Subhole, on your knees," SIR ordered.

I dropped. For an older guy he was hot.

"Does he drink from the tap?"

"Definitely. Whatever you want."

The Pisser unzipped his cod piece exposing a big floppy cock. A stream of warm yellow piss splattered across my chest. He aimed it so that it covered both pecs and my stomach.

Out of the corner of my eye I saw that SIR had turned to watch. "Hold that stomach in subhole. I trained you better than that."

The stream soaked my cock and pubic hair. Piss dripped down my thighs. The Pisser aimed higher, soaking my shoulders and neck. Then it hit my face.

"Open your mouth, boy," Pisser said.

I opened my mouth and warm piss filled the hole. I swallowed a bit but let most of it dribble out. Pisser stepped forward and shoved his semi-erect cock down my throat. He held the back of my head and skull fucked my face.

His cock grew to its full nine inch attention.

I opened wide and he fucked my face frantically.

That's when SIR moved in behind me and stuck HIS cock in my ass and pounded me hard.

The two of them fucked my holes and my body rocked as though I were the middle of some tug of war battle.

The Pisser moaned, "Oh yeah. He is well trained. Shit! I'm gonna fuckin' shoot my load. Ugh. Ugh. Yeah. Yeaaah."

Then the Pisser stood still while it was SIR's turn to shoot. "Goddamn piss hole. Cock suckin', subhole. Fuck. I'm gonna shoot. Fuck. Piss hole. Cock sucker. Yeah. Ughh. Yeah."

"Thank you, SIR," I said.

"Yes. Thank you." the Pisser said to SIR then left.

"Good work subhole."

Before the desert sun could dry the piss on my body I heard a voice from behind us. "It's nice to see the both of you again."

It's the bearded guy and his slave from the Tool Shed.

"How are you men doing?" SIR responded.

"Well, thanks. Having a great weekend. Definitely coming back next year," the Beard said.

"We always enjoy ourselves," SIR added with a sly smile.

"I assume you both have had enough sex. Though standing over here tells me it might not be too much just yet."

SIR glanced over to me. "The boy still needs some serving."

"I'd be happy to whip him into shape," the Beard said eagerly. "He's one hot slave. May I examine your property?"

"Absolutely," SIR said. "Whatever you want him to do."

The Beard stood in front of me and teased my nipples. "Nice big nipples." He squeezed them tighter.

"Ohh." I looked up at this man. Close-up, the Beard had quite an imposing presence. "Thanks, Master."

"He likes that," Beard said then twisted them and yanked 'em some more.

"Thank you, Master," I moaned.

"I could enjoy whipping you."

My SIR placed the gym bag next to the Beard and opened it. "Have your way with him."

Beard reached into his vest pocket and pulled out a pair of nipple clips and clamped them on my tits. The initial sharp pain spread across my chest and down my groin. My dick shot out, hard and prone.

"Thank YOU Master," I said. "Thank YOU SIR," I shouted.

Beard looked into the bag and took out the restraints. "Slave, put these on him."

He pulled out the riding crop and the flogger. "Hook 'em behind his back." The Beard pulled on the clamps and twisted them roughly.

The pain shot across my body and I closed my eyes and tilted my head up. "Oh yeah. Thank YOU Master."

"Oh yeah. I am going to enjoy this." He hit my chest with the back of his hand, causing the clamps to jiggle.

It startled me, momentarily.

"What do you say subhole?" my SIR asked.

"Thank you, SIR." This is gonna be intense, I thought to myself, a bit of apprehension setting in.

"Took you long enough. SIR taught you better." My SIR reprimanded me.

"Yes SIR."

Beard hit the other pec the same way.

My head jerked, again. "Thank You Master."

"Good slave," Beard said. "Down on your knees. Let me feel your tongue on my crotch."

"Yes SIR. Thank You Master." My tongue glided across Beard's smooth leather pants.

He pushed my head into HIS crotch and my face warmed quickly. Then he unbuckled the belt and opened the area exposing a jock strap. "Suck it up slave. Suck it up good."

I licked his jock and opened wide to let it in my mouth. It definitely smelled and tasted raunchy but not recently wet. "Thank You Master."

His cock sat inside the pouch and I opened wide and took it all in.

When he pulled the pouch away his uncut cock dangled freely. Its foreskin was thick. "Open wide slave."

I opened my mouth and Beard shoved the skin inside. It tasted nasty but it turned me on and I wanted more of Beard's raunchy cock.

"You like that nasty cock, slave?"

I grunted. "Yes Master. Thank YOU Master."

"He's a nasty raunch pig," my SIR yelled out, obviously enjoying this.

"He sure is," Beard said.

His big cock escaped from its cover and hit the back of my throat. Beard held my head down upon his tool. My breathing slowed and I held my breath. When I gasped Beard released his hold.

"Thank You Master." I gulped for air.

"Yeah, eat that cock, fucker. You got a HOT slave," Beard shouted to my SIR.

"Hear that subhole? What do you say to your SIR?"

"Thank you, SIR," I calmly said, still catching air.

"That's right. Are you a grateful subhole? Getting Master's ripe nasty cock down your throat." My SIR demanded to know.

"Yes SIR. Thank YOU SIR."

Then the Beard said, "Hook him up slave. Master feels sadistic."

"Yes Master," slave replied.

"Stand up boy," Beard said to me, reaching a hand out to help me up.

Slave guided me over to the cross beams and hooked my wrists to the eye bolts with my back facing out.

"What do you say subhole?" my SIR asked.

Even though Master Beard turned me on I felt nervous and exposed. "Thank YOU, SIR." I hoped I could handle him.

My SIR placed a blindfold on me. This helped block out the visuals of anyone who might be watching.

There's a quiet calm before the storm.

"Ready subhole," my SIR said.

"Yes SIR," I replied.

Beard ran the flogger across my back causing me to jerk a bit.

"Nothing you can't handle stud boy. Just breathe. Master's gonna use you for a while. Your SIR is right there. HE won't let anything happen that you can't handle."

"Yes Master." I knew he was right about that and it relaxed me a bit.

"That's a good boy."

I didn't feel him behind me anymore.

The flogger hit my back gently.

"Thank you, Master," I softly said.

It hit again and my back heated up.

"Get over here slave and get Master's cock primed. There's a hole it's gonna fuck real soon."

"Yes Master," slave said.

The flogger slapped against my shoulders, stinging.

"Uhh. Thank you Master."

"Suck that cock, slave. Master is getting horned up. A few more whips and I'll be ready to fuck that ass."

"Oh yeah," I moaned, eager for Beard's cock.

Another strike ripped into the skin of my shoulder.

"Thank you Master."

"Stick that ass out for me, subhole," Beard said, using the name SIR calls me. "I want it red when I fuck it."

"Yes Master."

"Do as he says, subhole. Stick that ass out," my SIR echoed from the side.

"Yes SIR." I extended my legs out, exposing more of my ass to Beard.

Smack! The leather snapped against my firm muscle butt.

"Thank you, Master." This action is more to my comfort zone. I inhaled deeply.

It struck again, harsher.

"Oh yeah. Thank you Master."

"You like that slave. Don't you?"

"Yes Master." Beard could do anything he wanted to my ass.

"You want a few more before I shove my cock up there?"

"Yes Master. Please Master. More."

"Then stick that ass out for me. Show me how badly you want it."

I extended it all the way, surrendering my ass and hole to Beard.

Sting! "Ooh!"

Smack! "Ouww."

Strike! "Ooh. Thank YOU Master." I couldn't extend my body any lower.

"I want that ass red before I fuck it," Beard roared.

"Yes Master," I cried out.

Three more strikes and Beard stopped.

My ass burned.

"Nice. Look at how red it is. It's fuckin' glowing like a campfire. Now I want to fuck it."

"Thank You, Master."

Beard stood close behind me. I felt his enormous presence and his warm breath. Fingers prodded my eager hole. I love getting fucked when I'm strung up.

"Yeah, nice hole. I'm gonna fill it and fuck it hard," Beard whispered in my ear.

"Oh yeah. Thank YOU Master."

"You want Master's cock, boy?"

"Yes Master. I do."

The tip of his cock set against the opening of my hole. "Here it is boy. You ready?" Beard drove forward. "It's all yours."

"Uugh. Yeah." It was big and tore into my hole. It hurt but felt fuckin' awesome."Thank YOU Master," I whispered, in agonized delight.

Beard shoved it in deeper and it felt like he was ripping me apart. I relaxed my body and took pleasure in the dual sensations. "Thank YOU Master. Ohh yeah."

He drew out slightly and thrust further back in. He battered my ass like a jack hammer, raping it harder and deeper than before.

"Oohh. Yes Master. Thank You Master." I couldn't get enough.

"Yeah. You like Master's big cock in your ass boy?"

"Yes Master. I do. Thank YOU Master," I groaned in painful pleasure.

Beard must have liked it too because now he fucked faster, brutally hitting that spot deep in there. The spot that hurts and feels good all the same. "Fuck! boy. Master likes fuckin' this ass."

"Oohh. Yeah. Fuck. Yeah." Each pounding sent sensations up and down my body. "Thank YOU Master." I held my ass out for HIS total use and pleasure. He rammed his raunchy cock deep inside me. It hurt but made me want more.

Suddenly, he popped his cock out, leaving me startled and dazed, my hole empty. I wasn't sure what had happened.

And then Smack! Slash! The flogger ripped across my ass cheeks. "I want that ass red when I fuck it," Beard bellowed, not bothering to set a pattern or rhythm. He just whaled away.

"Uugh."

Beard drilled his huge uncut cock deep inside my ass again.

"Ohh yeah. Thank YOU Master."

He drew it out and plowed deep in again, tearing my hole apart.

"Oohh fuck yeah. Thank you," I groaned hoarsely.

Then he yanked free again, leaving me cockless.

Slash! Across my ass.

"Get over there slave. Suck his cock. I want him to shoot just before I do."

Hearing this nearly made me explode. I hoped not too much sooner as my ass tightened after cumming. That's probably the whole point. But that might be too much after all this.

Slave's mouth gripped my cock like a fucking vacuum suck pump and no wonder, I thought, after the training he'd gotten impaled to Beard's enormous cock. I wanted to push him away to delay my ejaculation since it's never as good after you cum. But slave's expert ability just made my ass hungrier. Then slave's fingers were twisting the clamps on my nipples and I knew I was in trouble.

I stuck my ass out as far as it would go, accepting the inevitable outcome that my cock was going to shoot soon and my ass continued to be fucked. I might as well get the most pig pleasure and accept the onslaught of Beard's big cock ripping apart my tightened hole.

Smack! The crop hit my cheeks again.

Whack! Smack!

Master Beard's cock plowed in and rammed deep, out and back it drove while slave sucked my dick to full attention.

I lowered my body, gluttonously, "Oh yeah. Thank you Master. Fuck my hole."

He drove deep and his body slammed against mine. He reversed and banged full throttle. He was like a wrecking ball, propelling forward, furiously. "Fucking slave, fuck hole, taking Master's big raunchy cock."

I couldn't hold out any longer. "Uugh. OOhh." My body twisted and turned as I blew my load into slave's wet warm mouth.

Master Beard grabbed my waist and smashed into me like a rouge twelve rig crashes a brick wall.

"Ooh yeah. Fuckin' faggot ass fucked slave. Uugh. Shit. Fuck. Take Master's fuckin' load. Aahh."

His brute force nearly knocked me over. It's a good thing his sturdy slave was there to keep me upright.

Beard had driven up my tightened burning hole and he remained there. Slowly he caught his composure and stepped back. His cock slipped out of my loose, wet, used and sore hole.

"Now suck it out of him slave. Get Master's load back."

Shit. Now what? My ass was sore enough. I just wanted to get down. I hoped SIR would intervene but I didn't hear a word of protest. HE must be enjoying this.

Slave's mouth was on my ass lips before I knew it. He sucked my hole like my cock – Good!

"Ohh. Ohh," I cried out, wanting this to be over.

"Feed it to him, subhole. Give him what he wants." It's my SIR's voice.

"Shit," I mumbled.

"Push it out fuckhole. Feed him his Master's seed," Master Beard said. "Don't deny my slave his duty."

I tried to relax. Slave sucked and stuck his tongue in my wide loose rose bud. I pushed out hoping it would help and end this. It seemed an eternity. Some liquid moved.

"Oh yeah," I moaned. More fluids shifted. "Oh yeah."

Slave sucked on my hole. Normally this might turn me on but I was really over it and the clamps on my nipples hurt, not in a good way.

More fluid squirted out. I couldn't take anymore."Ouww, my ass. My ass. It's sore."

"You got it all slave. That's enough," his Master shouted.

"Yes SIR." Slave stopped and stepped away.

After a brief moment, I felt my hands released from the hooks. I collapsed backwards into someone's arms. I heard a voice in my ear. "Good work subhole." It was my SIR. HE propped me up with HIS arms and removed the clamps and my blindfold.

When I regained my vision I saw a crowd had formed around the cross. SIR grabbed the tool bag and led me through the crowd. They parted and let us through, suddenly breaking into applause.

———————

Back at the house SIR put me in the bed. I watched HIM moving around the room, packing up HIS things. HE sat down next to me on the bed and for the first time I felt HIS lips on mine. "Good boy, subhole. I'll see you next week."

"Yes SIR. Thank YOU SIR. My only purpose is to please the SIR."

I heard his truck pull out of the driveway as I drifted off to sleep.

ABOUT THE AUTHOR

My Ascent Into Submission is Nick Williams' first erotic novel. His stories have been published in Manifest Reader, Manhood Rituals, and Afterwords: Real Sex from Gay Men's Diaries. Nick Williams is a pen name.

His political essays and columns have been published in The Desert Sun, The Desert Times, The Bottom Line, IN LA Magazine, The Bay Area Reporter, The Press Democrat, We The People, and West County Times.

For the past seven years, Nick has lived in the land of never ending sunshine, Palm Springs; after ten years under the shade of towering redwoods along the Russian River. He moved to San Francisco in 1976, still a teenager at 19.

The first bar he snuck into was The Bolt. In those more carefree days of the 70's, there was never a doorman and the older leather crowd greeted the handsome sailor-looking, under age boy, with open arms. Nick was hooked from the start and never looked back. For you newcomers, the more modern name for The Bolt is The Powerhouse.

Soon after, a friend gave him a leather vest. To keep warm on those cold San Francisco summer nights he bought a Leather Motorcycle Jacket at Hard On Leather on Polk Street. He still treasures the jacket though after many years of working out, it no longer fits. His first, and still-fitting chaps, were from Leather Forever on 18th Street near Castro.

Nick Williams is currently working on several projects: the story of rescuing his Golden Retriever, who came to him in poor shape; the story of taking care of his former partner in the early 80's; putting together a collection of his columns and essays, and a collection of his erotic stories and tributes to the men who taught him and touched his life.

www.ingramcontent.com/pod-product-compliance
Lightning Source LLC
Chambersburg PA
CBHW070826250626
47170CB00006B/2224